Tonight, by Sea

A Richard Jackson Book

Tonight, by Sea

A NOVEL BY

Frances Temple

Orchard Books • New York

ACKNOWLEDGMENTS

Thanks to singer/poet Manno Charlemagne and to the groups
Boukman Eksperyans and Boukan Ginen for the wealth of
their songs.

Thanks to President Jean-Bertrand Aristide for the vision shared
in his books, *In the Parish of the Poor: Writings from Haiti*
(Maryknoll, New York: Orbis Books, 1990), *Aristide: An
Autobiography* (Maryknoll, New York: Orbis Books, 1993),
and in his speeches.

Thanks to Rose Marie Chierici for friendship and vivid stories.

Thanks to people in Haiti and the Dominican Republic whose
lives are lessons in generosity and risk, and especially to Amelia,
Sylvius, Sadrak, Coligny, and Milagros.

Orchard Books, 95 Madison Avenue, New York, NY 10016

Manufactured in the United States of America
Book design by Mina Greenstein
The text of this book is set in 12 point Aldus.
10 9 8 7 6 5 4 3 2 1

Library of Congress Cataloging-in-Publication Data
Temple, Frances. Tonight, by sea : a novel / by Frances Temple.
p. cm. "A Richard Jackson book"—Half title p.
Summary: As governmental brutality and poverty become
unbearable, Paulie joins with others in her small Haitian village to
help her uncle secretly build a boat they will use to try to escape to
the United States.
ISBN 0-531-06899-4.   ISBN 0-531-08749-2   (lib. bdg.)
[1. Haiti—History—1986-   —Fiction. 2. Blacks—Haiti—
Fiction.] I. Title.   PZ7.T244To 1995 [Fic]—dc20 94-32167

To Zetwal, Ti Bob, and Maribel

To the students of Mèt Beliar,
with high hopes for the lives
they will lead and the stories
they will write

TM

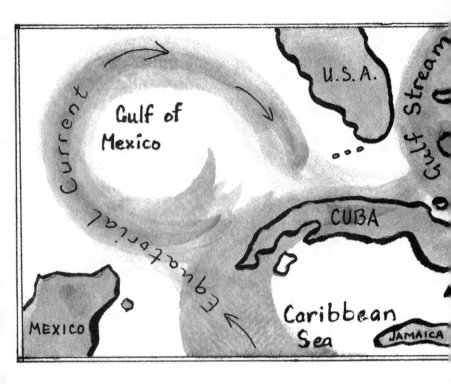

CONTENTS

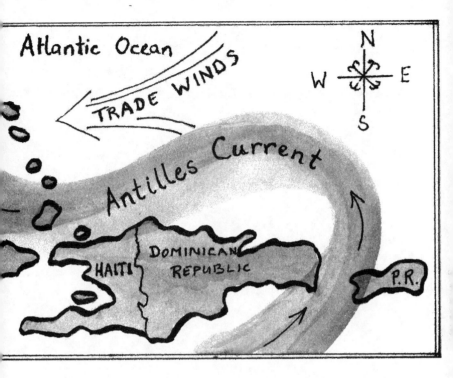

1

Ember

Kneeling in the sand, Paulie shredded dry seaweed and fluffed it into a heap between the three black cooking stones, half forgetting that she had no food to cook. She broke palm fronds over the seaweed, then propped two pieces of driftwood with their tips just above the palm. Raking the sand together with her fingers, she built up a ring around the outside of the stones, careful to make room for the air to blow in and give life to the fire, a little and not too much.

Paulie leaned back, still kneeling, circling her upper arms in her hands to warm them. Night had come. The tree frogs stopped singing all at once.

"You got matches, Uncle?"

Paulie's Uncle was washing in seawater from a bucket, pouring it down his back to get off the sweat and sawdust, rinsing his arms.

"All the matches gone, Paulie."

"Go see if you can borrow a coal," her grandmother said. Sitting on the step of her house, a cloth pulled around her thin shoulders, Grann Adeline leaned toward the fire as if it were already lit. She frowned, slapped at a mosquito on her ankle. "Go on, girl. Ask sweetly and somebody bound to give you an ember."

Paulie wandered down the sand path. The small houses clustered under the trees were mostly dark. She could hear voices talking softly, a baby crying. A thin dog came out and sniffed at the backs of her knees. Paulie looked for the glow of a cook fire, smelled the breeze for one. She could feel the sea air, and hear the waves coming in, but it seemed like nobody was cooking.

If Uncle had fifty *sentim*, she could go to the store and buy a pack of matches, enough for many fires. . . .

Uncle was a coffin maker by trade, and he had work. The tap-tapping of his hammer was like birdsong, heard every day, so frequent you forgot to notice it. Belle Fleuve had lost three children since last market: Zetwal, Ti Bob, Maribel. Hunger had weakened them and a passing fever had carried them away. But Uncle never had it in his heart to accept money for building a child-coffin. And anyway, today he was beginning work on a boat.

Paulie saw a flicker of orange at the bend in the road where her friend Karyl lived. Good. Almost everybody in Belle Fleuve was like family, but she and Karyl were two fingers on the same hand.

Paulie slipped carefully through the cactus fence that grew around Karyl's yard.

"*Bonswa*, Lucille, Karyl, Gabriel. Grann Adeline sent me to ask can she borrow one coal? Our fire ready to go except we don't have match. . . . Thank you, yes? Put it on this shell and I run fast. Thank you . . . bless . . ."

Paulie didn't stay long. Karyl and her family were eating. Paulie kept her eyes from their bowls, but she could smell sweet potato steaming.

Paulie ducked past Karyl's mother, smiling, sheltering the coal with her hand. "Thank you, Lucille, good-night. I must go because Grann wants to cook." She said this so Lucille would not feel pressed to invite her.

On the dark path, she stepped on a sea-almond and picked it up with her toes. It was only the husk, and she threw it back on the ground. Most days she went to the rocks close by the water and found a mussel or two, or some seaweed that filled their bellies so she and Uncle and Grann could sleep. But today had slipped by. Sweet potato boiled with milk would be so good, so good. . . .

Paulie took a big gulp of air to clear away the

dream of sweet potato. People knew Uncle was too busy to farm or to fish, the earth so dry now, the fish so scarce it took a lot of time and patience. And Uncle wouldn't get paid to work on the boat. Because really nobody had money, none of the people in Belle Fleuve who needed a small boat to leave Haiti. People would help however they could, though. Share food if they had it. Nobody begged in Belle Fleuve.

Passing a gap in the palms, Paulie looked out over the restless sea. Her parents, mother and father both, were across the water. Gone to find Life. It was a long time now since Grann Adeline had received a cassette tape or money order from them. Paulie peeked under her hand at the ember in the shell. She blew on it gently to make sure it was still live, and it glowed red in answer.

"Paulie, wait up!"

She jumped. Whose voice? Jean-Desir, Karyl's big brother, was walking after her on the path.

He was holding something. *Bondye*, she prayed, make it a sweet potato.

Paulie turned toward him, holding the shell close, a smile creeping across her face, the wind whipping her short dress. She could see what he held: a fish.

Paulie was a little afraid of Jean-Desir, now that he was almost grown. He didn't play with her and Karyl. Teacher had lent him a radio and he had kept it glued to his ear all year, barely speaking to the smaller children. Instead, he practiced the language of Radio Mee-ya-mee, repeating things he heard on the air, hard songs that sounded like somebody hitting in anger, making sharp explosive pops with his lips. And he had a magazine with pictures of naked women under his mattress: he had slapped Karyl for pulling it out.

Paulie tried not to think of this while she waited for him to offer his gift.

Jean-Desir held his arm straight toward her, dangling the fish at a safe distance from his clean shirt.

"*Bonswa*, Paulie! Lucille says to ask if Adeline can use this fish while he still fresh."

"*Respè*, Jean-Desir. Tell your mama thank you, yes, we will cook and eat the fish with pleasure this very night."

"Can I walk with you?"

Nobody had ever asked Paulie such a question.

"The path is mine?" she asked, and Jean-Desir laughed with a flash of teeth.

"You some little girl, Paulie!"

When Jean-Desir gave Paulie his admiring look, she lost some of her worry.

"Not *so* little, Jean-De." She called him by his mother's nickname on purpose. "Well, hurry, man, before this coal die out."

It was pleasant to walk along together in the night, hearing the sea uncurl along the shore.

Back at Grann Adeline's, Paulie tucked the ember under the seaweed. On all fours, she blew steadily until a flame caught, then sat back on her heels, content to feel the fire flicker on her face.

Adeline cleaned the fish. She put its head separate in a pan of water to make soup. She split the body into two flat pieces and lifted out the backbone. She put the pieces in the frypan to cook, and propped the pan on the cooking stones over the fire.

Jean-Desir waited.

Neither Grann nor Uncle said much, and Paulie thought maybe it was because they were so tired. But maybe also it was because they had seen Jean-Desir laughing with the soldiers, the *macoutes* who prowled among them, took their chickens, beat up the teacher so there could be no more school. One of the soldiers had a motorcycle, he even had gasoline, and everyone had seen Jean-Desir riding behind the soldier as if they were friends.

"Tell your mama, Jean-Desir, we thank her for this fine fish," Adeline said finally.

Jean-Desir smiled and nodded quickly. "She only too glad, yes?" But he didn't leave. He turned instead to Paulie's uncle. "I understand you building a boat, Uncle."

Uncle said nothing.

"That one difficult job, not so?"

Uncle shrugged, looking embarrassed, and squatted by the fire.

"How much time do this work take, Uncle?" Jean-Desir asked.

Uncle reached his hands toward the fire, turning them as if they were cold. "That's hard to say, friend."

Uncle called many people friend, but Paulie felt a question in his voice this time.

Jean-Desir looked over his shoulder, then dropped beside Uncle and spoke in a murmur. "I heard on the radio, last night the *macoutes* stopped a boat was leaving from Isle La Tortue. I hear they killed more than thirty people with machine gun. . . ."

Paulie looked out to the sea, imagining ghost people floating on the water. She moved closer to the fire, to Grann. Jean-Desir stood and spoke again, more loudly, in a cheerful voice. "If I have luck, I'll bring another fish tomorrow."

"*Si Dye vle*. We thank you, Jean-Desir. Tell your mama Lucille sleep well."

"Good-night, then. Sweet dreams, Paulie."

When Jean-Desir was well down the path, Paulie looked up at Uncle to see what he was thinking. His kind face was bunched up in a knot of worry.

"We can trust the boy?" he asked, looking in the fire. Paulie felt confused. Uncle had known Jean-Desir since he was born. Why did he ask her?

Jean-Desir could be mean, but so could Karyl, sometimes. So could Paulie herself. Jean-Desir could be loud, yelling and singing. He could be so mean and moody nobody could talk to him. . . . "*Li mete chapo djab, jodia*," the children of Belle Fleuve would say, with a shrug. "He's wearing the devil's hat just now." They all fought and made up ten times a day.

We can trust the boy?

She wished she could answer yes, for sure.

A saying of Grann's came into her mind: You can measure a snake only when it is dead. Paulie shivered. She wondered if she was catching a fever.

She laid another dry palm frond on the fire. The fish began to steam.

"How was the day?" she asked Uncle, to make talk. "Did you begin the boat for true?"

Uncle reached over and picked up the fish bone Adeline had removed. He ran his finger down the center.

"See that, Paulie? On a boat, they call that keel. Today we made the keel. Tomorrow . . ." Uncle had a smile that crinkled his whole face and made his eyes shine in the firelight. He cupped the fish bone in his hands, pressing the spines up on either side of the backbone. "Tomorrow, we start the ribs."

2

Kok Chante

Daybreak. Paulie woke to a loud rooster crow. The rooster himself was walking back and forth beside her cot, preening, stretching his neck.

"Scare me one more time like that and I tell Grann we eat you with coconut," Paulie said, swinging her legs over the side of the cot and pulling on her braids to make them sit high on her head.

The rooster looked at her with a proud round eye, strutted to the door, and hopped down into the yard. Paulie sang a note for each familiar thump, as the rooster hit two wooden steps and then the sand.

> "Kok chante
> Fo chanje"

The refrain ran through her head. Rooster sing, changes bring. . . . The rooster had scared her out of her sleep, all right. No drifting back into that nice dream now. Paulie shook her head and reached for her dress. Rooster knew as well as Paulie did, Grann would never eat him.

Paulie craned to see outside and glimpsed a little sun on the top of the palm trees.

It felt like the right time to be walking down the road, going to school. She wondered where her teacher, Mèt Sadrak, was just now. She missed his broken-tooth smile, his worried, enthusiastic look, his chalk-whitened hands gesturing in the air as he tried to explain this and that. She missed the excitement of school, even the effort of sitting so straight on the benches.

Mèt Sadrak had taught the school two whole years with only smiles for pay, Grann said. A good man, though plenty strict. But last week the *macoutes* had come, yelling about how Mèt Sadrak was "Lavalas," and dragged him out of the school shed. One man wasn't in uniform, but he had a gun anyway, and an armband that said FRAPH. Paulie saw him beat Mèt Sadrak with twin slaps on the face, making his head jerk back again and again. All the children were crying. The *macoutes* fired guns in the air. She and the other children ran home, and when they came back again, they found a sign on the school shed saying, THIS SCHOOL IS CLOSED DOWN BY ORDER OF THE PROVISIONAL GOVERNMENT OF HAITI. It was a printed sign. Paulie heard Grann's friends say signs like that were going up everywhere.

"What is so bad about Lavalas?" Paulie asked Grann, first chance she got.

"Lavalas is a flood," Grann said.

"I know that," said Paulie, exasperated. "But Mèt Sadrak, he sure is no flood!"

"One drop of rain doesn't make a flood," said Grann.

Then Paulie remembered words she had heard, before the time of trouble, when Father Aristide was President of Haiti:

Yon sèl nou feb
Ansanm nou fò
Ansanm ansanm nou sé lavalas.

Alone we are weak
Together we are strong
Together together we are the flood.

In school, people worked together. Mèt Sadrak saw to that. *"Tet ansanm,"* he would say. "You and you, put your heads together and find a solution to this problem."

So maybe that was why the *macoutes* busted up the school.

Paulie didn't realize she had sighed so loud until Grann said, "Stop messing with your notebook and grieving about school. Go see if Uncle can use your help, down on the beach."

"*T*onnè!" said Uncle. "These boats not at all like coffin. These blasted boats have line like palm tree, nothing straight. . . ."

On the hard part of the sand he had laid out a series of planks, overlapping them to make twelve curved pieces that would become the ribs of the boat. Behind them, down the beach, some few palm trees strayed toward the water. Paulie saw that the curves of the palms matched those of a finished boat, almost straight awhile, then coming round fast.

"Why you don't use the palm tree itself to build this boat, Uncle?" she asked.

"Wood too punky, is why," Uncle said. He was piling boards beside the keel, trying to figure how there could be enough to make a boat. "Palm wood soak up the ocean water, fast, *ssssip*. Water make palm puff like sponge. Then the boat become heavy, Paulie, maybe even sink. . . . Even house boards better than palm for building a boat." Uncle frowned. He stood and stretched, his hands on his hips. Then he picked up his hammer. "Why you don't go see if you can help Sauveur, down by his house?"

Up and down the beach Paulie looked, in among the trees, at the houses painted green, pink, turquoise. Little houses with wobbly tables half-sunk in the sand between them, where men played dominoes to pass the time when they had no work.

Since forever Paulie had been seeing the same little houses, nestled in under the palms. Every day of her life she had run in and out of those houses of Belle Fleuve, trying to smell if anyone was roasting coco-bread.

Today, following Uncle's gaze, she looked for their friend Sauveur. There he was, a dusty-skinned gangly man with his hat pulled low over his ears. As she watched, he took hammer and crowbar and pulled his house down. Just a creak and sigh: the nails slid out, the boards knocked loose. Sauveur stacked boards to carry them to Uncle. Paulie ran to help, dragging a board in each hand and following in Sauveur's footsteps.

"Where will you sleep when the rains come?" she asked.

Sauveur stopped, balancing a pile of boards on his shoulder, and looked up at the flat blue sky.

"Don't know if the rains are coming at all this year, Paulie."

Her face must have shown fright, because Sauveur made one of his clown faces at her, dropping his jaw long, closing his eyes halfway until he looked like a turtle. He put his free hand on his chest. "Tell your heart don't jump so, sweetie," he said. "The way things are now, you can have house, or you can have boat, but you can't have both."

"Why is that?"

Sauveur raised his eyebrows. "Because, *kòkòt*, there's not much wood in Haiti anymore." He smiled at her, but his face looked sad as he turned away, circling his boards with both hands and lowering them to the sand.

"Why do you have stripes on your legs, Sauveur?" She had never noticed before that he had stripes, like bruises or rope burns. Sauveur was leaning over, stacking the boards. His hat fell to the sand, and Paulie dropped her boards and clapped a hand over her mouth. Sauveur's head was naked as an eggplant.

"Enough question, girl!" Uncle pressed an empty paint can into Paulie's hand. "Your job be to pull nails from these boards, and when you done pulling them all, take this hammer and pound each one straight. If you don't know how, I show you."

"All right, yes, Uncle," Paulie said. Pulling nails would take her mind off the empty space where Sauveur's house had been, and the sad, naked look of Sauveur's head.

*M*ore than working, Paulie liked watching Uncle work, his white T-shirt flapping like a flag against his ribs. He was thin. You could see how his bones joined up, and the flat muscles that changed the patterns under his skin when he lifted the hammer. Sometimes he paused in his work, still as a lizard, his fingertips resting on the wood. In those moments, Paulie held her breath. Uncle was waiting for understanding. When it came, he would begin work again, understanding guiding his hands.

Paulie thought how lucky she was that her mother and father had given her to Uncle and to Grann Adeline to raise, when they went across the water. Before that, when Uncle was a boy, he had a different name. But people said that once Paulie came, she followed him everywhere calling, "Uncle! Uncle!" until everybody forgot his other name and called him Uncle, too.

*W*hen the sun fell low enough to glow through the green of the breakers, Grann Adeline came looking to see if anything to eat had fallen or washed up on the shore.

"Girl . . . ," she said, settling beside Paulie, tucking her skirt between her knees. She sorted through the nails her granddaughter had collected with a critical expression.

"You hear what happened to the boy's hair?" she asked around the straightened nails she had stuck between her teeth.

"What boy?" Paulie asked, alarmed.

"That boy," said Grann, jerking her chin up the beach. "Sauveur."

Paulie laughed. "He's not a boy, Grann. Sauveur just about as old as Uncle!" She hammered a nail against a rock. It kept flipping over. *"Tonnè!"* she muttered. "So what happened to his hair, eh, Grann?"

"He went into town last night. Some *macoutes* rough him up. Shave the hair from his head."

"Why?" Paulie asked. "*Li simpatik.* Everybody likes Sauveur."

Grann took the nails from between her teeth and pursed her lips.

"Know how he used to go to class in town, learning letters?"

Paulie thought about it. "Same class Uncle went to, yes?"

Grann nodded. "Well, seems that the *macoutes* remember he went to that class. *Macoutes* say if he want to read, he must be Lavalas. He must support the little priest. . . ."

"So they beat him up?"

"*Eh wi,*" said Grann. She held a crooked nail in the air. "This one need some work."

3

The Seek Life Kombit

Paulie and Uncle got to the beach so early there was still a haze on the water. The sky was purple as a shell. The air carried the smoky smell of last night's cook fires.

Uncle looked at the keel, the stacks of planks, the stumps set in loose sand, and shook his head.

"Paulie," he said, "let's you and me move all this to the riverbed. Ground is harder there and we be a little more out of sight."

The riverbed was lower than the rest of the beach, grown up in Congo grass. The firm sand, mixed with earth, felt cool to Paulie's toes. Some big rocks were scattered about; leaning across one, she noticed its top was damp with dew and pressed her tongue against it until the moisture was gone.

"This was the riverbed, Uncle?" she asked. She rolled her tongue in her mouth. "The river Belle Fleuve came down right here?"

Uncle nodded. He was setting up a workbench, two planks across two rocks, and squinting to see if it was even. "Your papa and I did swim where you standing. River water did push us bumpety-bump into the sea."

"Cool," said Paulie, in English. It was a word they'd all learned from Jean-Desir, who used it frequently.

"*Koul ampil,*" said Uncle. "Plenty cool." He smiled.

Paulie lined up his tools on the workbench—a hammer, a big saw, a little saw, a chisel. She made a line of the nails that were ready to use, turning them at angles to one another so they would look like they were dancing.

"Pretty," said Uncle. "A *fèt* of nails. Now you come help with this."

Together, one at each end, they dragged the keel over and propped it between rocks. They arranged the planks of wood by size, ready to use.

Paulie was sitting on a rock, watching the sun balancing on the eastern horizon, when Uncle's friend Mondestin came down the beach with his girlfriend, Mireille, and her mother. Uncle stopped work, put a finger to his lips, and winked at Paulie. She held her breath, waiting to see if the boat work would be noticed. Mireille and her mother walked past down near the water, talking. Suddenly they backed up, waved, and came up the riverbed. Paulie let out her breath. Uncle shook his head and went back to work.

"That's not a coffin you building now, Uncle?" Mireille asked, mischief in her voice. "We just checking before we book passage."

"Won't see *me* going to Mee-ya-mee, U.S.A., in no coffin," added Mondestin, coming up behind her.

Uncle squatted in the sand, intent on fixing the keel smoother and stronger. At last he looked up at Mireille and her mother.

"Mornin', beautiful ones." He smiled and put his head to one side. "Can we keep this boat a secret?"

"Oh!" Mondestin, turning his visor cap backward, circled the woodpiles, the keel, the tool bench. "This is a boat? Look like a pile of bones to me."

Mireille threw back her head and laughed. "A secret in Belle Fleuve? Uncle. We are of each other's blood and we all breathe the same air, not so?"

Uncle stood, resting his foot on the keel of the boat, and patted it respectfully with his toes. A head shorter than Mondestin, he looked up at them from under his hat. The way he stood, so sure and calm while they teased him, made Paulie proud. With the hammer, she pulled a nail from a board, easing it out quietly.

"*Mezanmi*, my friends," Uncle said in his pleasant and serious way, "this is not coffin you see here.

This is no pile of bones. This here is the boat we build to seek life."

"Is that what we call her, Uncle, *Chache Lavi, Seek Life?*" Paulie asked.

"We could. . . ." Uncle bent to brush off the keel. He looked at the others. "What do you think?"

"*Souvenance,*" said Mireille's mother. It was her hometown, and the name rolled off her tongue like a blessing.

"*Unsinkable,*" suggested Mireille.

"Might be too much to hope," Mondestin said.

"*Hope,*" said Paulie. "*Espwa.*"

"*Zo Yo,*" said Mondestin. "*Bones.*"

"Hmmmm," Mireille said. "*Chache Lavi—Seek Life.* . . . Maybe that the best."

The older woman held out a hand to Mireille. "Come, daughter. Shellfish calling to us." They went on down the beach, swinging an empty bucket between them.

Mondestin stayed to help Uncle.

Under Uncle's chisel, Paulie could see fine lines of pink and turquoise and green. The rest of the paint from the boards that used to be Sauveur's house, up under the palms.

"*Belle Fleuve Seek Life,* Uncle? Since the boat for everybody?"

"Everybody seek life," said Uncle.

"That's true," said Paulie.

*P*aulie didn't know for sure who would sail on *Seek Life* if ever Uncle got through building it. But all that morning everybody who lived nearby along the beach in Belle Fleuve brought what they thought Uncle might use.

Lucille dumped some burlap bags and blue plastic next to Paulie. "Maybe he can piece them together for a sail."

Maribel's mother brought a bag of pig hair. "Maybe there will be cracks to fill, yes?"

Uncle shook his head, his nose wrinkling up as if he were about to sneeze, smiling and disagreeing at the same time. Paulie knew he was not planning to leave cracks.

Whoever sailed, in the end, *Seek Life* was everybody's.

Paulie heard a lot of talk about who would go over the water to find work and send money to Belle Fleuve. The talk was not about who wanted to go but about who was strongest, and ablest, and most likely to find paid work that would buy food to keep them all alive.

Sauveur brought the table that had been outside his house and set it in the sand not far from the boat, so that he and Mondestin could play dominoes until Uncle needed them. Paulie turned her paint can upside down and sat on it, close to the table.

"Uncle is strong," she heard Sauveur say, as the dominoes clicked. "Strong as we have, and smart with his hands. . . . Uncle could find work in the U.S.A."

These words made Paulie's heart jump with anxiety. Then Mondestin said, "Yeah, but Uncle is too kind, see. Uncle will give away money to anybody who ask, and then he have nothing left to send home money order to Belle Fleuve.''

Paulie wondered if this was maybe why they had not gotten any money from her parents.

"I think we need to send somebody more *biznisman*. . . .''

"Like maybe you own self, eh, Mondestin?''

Mondestin flipped a domino in answer, swept his bottle-cap winnings into a heap, and winked at Paulie.

"Why can't we all stay here?'' Paulie asked, resting her forehead on the edge of the table.

"We stay here, we going to starve,'' Mondestin said. "We going to starve because we have no government, no land, and no way to make a living.''

Sauveur put the dominoes back in the cigar box where he kept them. He and Mondestin got up and stretched. Mondestin had black, black skin and stood twice as tall as Paulie when he stretched. His white T-shirt had MARLBORO written across it in red letters. He pulled one of Paulie's braids.

"Look at this beautiful girl, her head so heavy with thinking, her neck thin as a flower stalk. . . . We can't let our Paulie starve, eh, Sauveur? We must take her over the waves and make her fat on Colonel chicken, yes?'' He lifted Paulie's chin gently with two fingers and looked her in the eye. "Is for our Paulie we will cross the waters.''

Paulie lowered her eyelids and tried to smile peacefully, tried to be calm and strong, but she could feel her heart jumping in circles.

22

Sauveur and Mondestin went to help Uncle by holding together the planks that made up the ribs of the boat while he nailed.

Paulie was glad to be left alone. She could not imagine living outside Belle Fleuve. She didn't want to think about which person would go and which person would stay, or about the great watery abyss that would separate them. But she did want to think about Mondestin's words and the touch of his fingers on her chin, to tuck the comfort of those things around her heart like a blanket. Not just Uncle, but Mondestin and Sauveur and them wanted to save her life. Her life was their life.

Maribel's mother had come down the beach, dragging her bag of pig hair to Uncle. Paulie looked for Maribel, who used to peek out from behind her mother's skirt, laughing because Paulie pretended to be surprised. Even though Paulie had followed the little white box to the graveyard, singing with all the people of Belle Fleuve, she forgot for a minute that Maribel had died. Just for lack of food.

Mondestin said that there was no food because there was no government.

Her teacher said their leader, Aristide, was in exile in the U.S.A. because the *macoutes* had made a coup d'état and forced him to leave. Careful people didn't speak his name out loud. They called Titid "the little priest," and spoke softly. But for a short while, when he was President, Haiti did have a government. . . .

Uncle and his friends had voted for Aristide to be President. Uncle had reminded her about it one night not long ago when they were waiting for rice to cook. Uncle had shown her a picture of Aristide that he kept hidden in his sleeping mat. That night, after he showed the picture to Paulie, he burned it. As it curled in the flames, Uncle had said, "The time we went and voted for Titid, *eh byen* . . . it was like a vote for we own selves, Paulie. Like trying to say, We can do it. *We* can make this little country work. You can understand that, Paulie?"

Still sitting on the paint can, her head resting on the table, Paulie thought about what Uncle had said. She thought about her friend Karyl's father who was hiding in the hills somewhere and hardly ever came home even to sleep. Then she got up and moved closer to Uncle and his friends. She listened to their talk so hard she forgot about clawing nails from boards. She pulled a leaf from her pocket and stuffed it in her mouth, chewing its bitterness. Sometimes when she went suddenly from happy to sad, it was good to chew on something. Grann Adeline gave her leaves to carry with her for when this happened.

What made her heart fall now was thinking that Uncle and his friends were being pushed from their own place, from Belle Fleuve. Weren't they good men? Shouldn't they be able to find life in Haiti, and sleep in their own beds?

Paulie opened her mouth to ask, pushing the wad of leaf to the side of her jaw and swallowing the juice. It made her stomach churn, and she waited to let it settle before speaking. While she was waiting, another thought came to her. *Some questions steal a person's courage. Maybe I won't ask.* So instead she said, "Tell me about this Florida you all talking about."

Uncle switched his hammer to his left hand and used his arm to wipe the sweat that was running down his forehead.

"*Lòt bò dlo,* the other side of water, Mee-ya-mee, U.S.A., Florida, all the same. People can find life there. Money leastways," he said.

"But your life not money, Uncle. Your life . . ." Paulie waved her hand. She wanted to say, Your life is *me.* And work, building a coffin or a boat, talking to friends. Grann always said, "The things you do, you should do out of love." Out of love, not for money.

Uncle looked up from where he was squatting, running nails diagonally through a finished rib into the keel. His eyes crinkled almost shut, his nose spread wide, his crooked teeth flashed in the sun. He pointed his finger at her and said, "You." Then he added, "Do you have straight nails for me yet, Paulie?"

Sauveur and Mondestin were still talking about *lòt bò dlo.* It was cold over there, they agreed.

4

FRAPH

 When Karyl's mama, Lucille, was in a rage, you could hear her shout way up to Grann's house. This morning her voice was shrill, fear in it like a knife. "You think maybe you a man because suddenly God give you long legs! You think maybe you got some special place in a high-up tree because you learn some foreign *bla-bla-bla* on the radio! Let me tell you, my son . . ."

Paulie hesitated on the path. She wanted to see if Karyl would come to the beach with her, but if she went to Karyl's now, she would be caught in the storm of Lucille's wrath. Besides, some arguments were for family alone. Paulie sat down outside of

Karyl's *lakou*, close to the cactus fence, and waited for Lucille to finish being mad.

"You join FRAPH and I won't know you again. No son of mine joins FRAPH," Paulie heard Lucille say, her voice suddenly low and cold. The very idea made Paulie jump. Jean-Desir join FRAPH? FRAPH was a *macoute* organization, part army, part hired thugs. They knifed people, shot people. They had beat up her teacher.

There was a murmur of reply from Jean-Desir.

"Speak to me straight, boy, or don't take my time with your talking!"

"I said, Maman, is *my* life we talking about, not yours."

"And who give you your life, then? What respect you got for your mother and father, then? Your father, honest farmer, organization leader, did go in hiding so you can join up with his enemies?"

Paulie began listening in earnest. Karyl never would talk about her father.

"My father chose his way. He can choose any way he wants. I am not angry with what he chooses, even though it does mean his family must live with nothing."

"What you mean, *nothing?*" Lucille asked, her voice rising again. "We live with what other people have. Life. Dignity. We don't join up with bullies. We don't sell our true self for cigarettes or magazines. Not even for food. We sooner die."

"Maman," Paulie heard Jean-Desir say. "Maybe I myself would sooner live."

There was a silence that rang in Paulie's ears. Then Lucille's voice, tentative, for once. "What about the boat? Do you want to go in Uncle's boat?"

Silence. Then Jean-Desir spoke again. "Don't know if they want me, Maman. . . . Anyway, you can't believe that *everybody* who joins up with FRAPH is evil—"

"Evil exists," said Lucille. "And FRAPH is evil."

"FRAPH is a bunch of poor devils trying to stay alive, Maman."

"Trying to stay alive by killing people is evil," said Lucille, so flatly that it made Paulie stand up, because she knew even Jean-Desir couldn't talk back to a truth like that.

Paulie held her breath a minute, then stepped into the compound. She was just in time to see Lucille whack the head off a fish, her machete coming down so fast and hard the fish head flew across the yard. Chickens ran squawking to peck at it.

"Morning, Lucille," said Paulie in a voice she tried to make casual. "Can Karyl come with me to the beach?"

"Show my girl how to swim good, eh, Paulie?" Lucille said softly. The machete still in her hand, she bit the skin on the back of her arm, looking at Paulie anxiously. Circles under her eyes were darker than the rest of her face.

"I will," Paulie promised. "Karyl can already float like a star in the sky, Lucille."

*O*n the beach, Uncle and Mondestin and Sauveur were joining the ribs of the boat with a rail made of spliced-together boards.

"What do you call that?" Paulie asked.

"Call that a gunwale," answered Uncle.

"Gunwale," Paulie repeated. "Looks like the top of a basket to me."

"Same thing, almost," said Uncle.

"Except we hope this basket float," said Sauveur.

Paulie and Karyl squatted nearby and began to play *oslè*, tossing and gathering pig bones. Paulie's fingers were long and quick, and at first she was winning. Then Karyl, with a look of fierce concentration on her face, gathered four, and shouted, "*Heh!* I beat you! I'm the finest! Look how you miss—"

"Girl," Uncle growled, "run away from here before I throw this hammer at you!"

"Catch me, Paulie!" called Karyl, sprinting across the sand to the ocean's edge. "You know something? You have one mean Uncle!"

Paulie ran and splashed into the water, ready to dunk Karyl. "Say *pa vre*, or you drown!"

"*Pa vre!*" Karyl shouted, spitting water. "Not true!" She came up so close that Paulie could see the water sparkling on her eyelashes. Her braids stood straight up, the water beading and running off them. Karyl put her forehead against Paulie's, turning her head this way and that. It made Paulie dizzy, like falling into a mirror. Karyl grinned at her, her eyes so close they crossed. Then she whispered, smiling,

"Your Uncle is going to let Jean-Desir go with him in *Seek Life*, not so?"

Paulie flipped onto her back, scared suddenly for Uncle and his boat. What if Jean-Desir had already joined FRAPH? What if he had reported Uncle to the *macoutes* for building a boat? Would the *macoutes* beat Uncle? Shave his head? Would they kill him?

Kicking hard, she splashed water all over Karyl, churning up a high, wide waterspout that hid her friend and the beach and the boat. In her mind, Paulie became a powerful whale, turning in the water, twisting free from worry.

5

Lakou

Paulie trailed behind Grann Adeline, who was wading in the sea near the rocks, searching for food. The sun caught the fine line of a piece of fishing filament snagged on the rocks. Paulie freed it carefully and wound it around a stick. Maybe they could use it for tying or sewing, maybe for fishing. She dropped the stick in her bucket.

"Look for those little purple mussels, Paulie. See if you don't find them clinging underneath the rock edge."

Paulie set down her bucket, stretched out on the wet rock, hung her head over the edge, and peered underneath. Behind a green trail of slime she saw a cluster of purple wing shells.

"Eh, Grann!" she called. "You amazing woman! You are smart as a hawk!" She lowered the bucket under the shells and carefully broke them free. They looked very small in the bottom of the bucket, but small food was better than no food.

Grann Adeline stood ankle-deep in water, her toes curled inward against the pull of the surf. She had her hands on her hips. "Leave some few so they can grow back," she called.

Paulie bit her lip. She had picked every one.

"Sorry, Grann. I got them already. Just a few there."

Grann Adeline sagged against a rock.

"You tired, Grann?" Paulie asked. She came to lean beside her grandmother, showing her what was in the bucket.

"I lose courage, is all," said Grann.

Paulie reached in her pocket for a leaf. Grann took it, tore off half, and chewed it slowly.

"Because of the shellfish, yes?" Paulie said.

"The shellfish too much like we own selves," said Grann, her eyes closed. She swallowed, and put a hand on Paulie's arm.

"How?" Paulie asked.

Grann was so long in answering, Paulie asked the question again. "What makes you say the shellfish like we, Grann?"

"When I was a girl like you, Paulie . . . You should have seen *lakou* then! Five houses grouped together! So many children everywhere!" Grann, her eyes still closed, held out her hands as if invisible children would run into them. "Then I was a mother, too, with children hanging on my skirt. At nighttime, four, five household gathering around the fire. Women turning cassava bread, cooking corn mash and beans. Men talking about the day out fishing, talking about currents and monster fish and narrow escape . . . Heh *heh*!" Grann laughed toward the sun, her eyes still closed. "Get away from me, I don't believe you!" she said warmly, and Paulie could tell that she was talking to someone far away in her past, someone she liked.

"*Lakou* . . . ," Grann repeated. "*Lakou* is the center for us, the rock we all cling on. And there were so many of us! Plenty, plenty, plenty! So close, just standing together we protect each other. The big hurricane come. We hold. The wind howl. The water rise up. We stand firm. Now . . ."

Slowly Grann opened her eyes and turned to Paulie. "Now we are so few. Too few to protect each other. Easy to brush us apart."

Paulie put her arms around her grandmother, feeling her sadness. Stiffly, neither comforting nor comforted, Grann continued.

"Your mama leave. Your daddy leave. Estimé, Orestin, Micheline, Destiné, Monespoir, all of them leave Belle Fleuve. One off to the city to find work. Another off to find him. Two more go cross the water. They send one, two cassette tape, then we hear nothing. . . . Estimé's house fall into the sand, then Micheline's. People drag off the boards. At night, one, two people around a fire . . ."

Grann shrugged Paulie away, and sucked her

teeth anxiously. She turned and faced the wet rock, both hands flat against it, her head low. Suddenly her shoulders relaxed and Paulie saw her grandmother's face transformed. A tiny crab, almost transparent, skittered between her hands.

Paulie made a move to capture it, but Grann took hold of her arm in a strong grip.

"Stop! Leave that little crab in peace. That crab—" She gazed out to sea, her face open to all the light that bounced off the waves in spiderweb patterns. "That crab is messenger. From all the ancestors that go before, from the dead in the deep-sea abyss."

Paulie bit her knuckles. She was glad Karyl wasn't with them. It embarrassed her when Grann's mind wandered so. She wanted to pull the talk back to a normal place. "They're still family, aren't they, Grann? My mama, my father, Estimé, all your brothers, they're still someplace, living, yes?"

"*Eh wi*. Living or dead, they still family. Is them that sent the messenger."

Paulie sighed. Was this craziness? But if Grann wanted to talk of a crab messenger, she must listen.

"What did he say, Grann?" she asked softly. "Tell me the crab's message."

Grann half closed her eyes and gazed far out into the blue sky. She puffed her cheeks twice, as if she still had her pipe.

"He says," Adeline said, "he tell me, 'Don't worry, beautiful Adeline. . . .' "

Paulie smiled. "He looked at you with his little eyes all poked out and said that?"

"That and more," answered Adeline. "He said, 'Don't worry, Adeline. Yes, people do leave *lakou*. Many more will leave, and perhaps there will be nobody at all standing in this place. That does not mean family is finished, Adeline. Wasn't your people scattered before, brought from Guinea/Africa as slaves? Didn't they keep ties of the spirit? Yes! And they your people. So now your people far, far away, and still they be linked, through rainbow and spider-web, through thought and *seremoni*. They going to stay together through the telephone and cassette tape and money order system. They are your people. Always. *Lakou* will hold.' "

"The little crab said all that, Grann?" She wished she hadn't scoffed. "Tell me again, Grann."

" '*Lakou* will hold,' " Grann repeated. "That's what he said."

Adeline lurched and sat against a wet outcropping of rock, her feet still in the water, ankle-deep in gravel. With a trembling hand, she reached into her head-tie and pulled out a leaf. She folded it twice and stuck it in her mouth, mashing it slowly to release its juice.

Paulie squatted in the water, rinsing the sand from tiny purple shellfish that twinkled in the sun like angel wings.

6
On Camera

When Paulie woke next morning, Uncle had already slipped out. By the time she finished sweeping the yard and fetching Karyl and got to the beach, Uncle and Sauveur and Mondestin were lifting the keel, the ribs, the gunwale, all in a piece. They flipped the boat skeleton upside down and carefully set it across two strong sections of palm, nice and even. Then Uncle climbed on another stump, held his chisel against the thickest part of the keel, and began carving a hole right through it.

Hand in hand, Karyl and Paulie watched.

"What's the hole for, Uncle?"

"Centerboard trunk," said Uncle.

Sauveur looked mysterious. Mondestin put his fists on his hips and grinned.

"For the centerboard," said Uncle.

"*Eh wi?*" said Paulie.

"Let's swim," Karyl said. "Check on it later."

*T*he midmorning sun was hot already.

Paulie held her hands under Karyl's back, then slowly, gently let go. Karyl stiffened and sank again, came up beating the water.

"How come I sink and you don't?" she said between coughs. "*Poukisa?*"

"You just need to lie in the water like you part of the water, Karyl, not like it's some kind of enemy. . . ."

Down the way was some commotion, a knot of people coming from the part of Belle Fleuve where the road touched the beach. Most were children. In the middle, they could see a white man with a black beard, a box balanced on his shoulder.

"*Jounalis!*" said Karyl in a whisper.

"Who told him about the boat?" Paulie asked.

Karyl shrugged. "Who told him about the swimming lesson?"

Hand in hand, the two girls came slowly out of the water to get a closer look at the stranger. He wore shorts and a shirt with button pockets like Jean-Desir's, and had hair growing on his legs. Karyl rubbed her leg and puffed her nostrils at Paulie, and Paulie stuck her tongue in her cheek. He carried a camera on his shoulder, one big eye in the front of a black plastic box. Over the big eye, a small red eye blinked off and on.

"Stand away from it," said Adeline, who had come down to the beach with the crowd. She pushed Paulie behind her.

"Why? Is not a gun, eh, Grann?"

"Is not a gun, but it can bring trouble just the same."

The men at the riverbed greeted the cameraman with tight nods. They kept working, in a stiff way that was not natural to them. Paulie thought the *jounalis* should ask permission to take pictures of their work, but he didn't. Uncle and Sauveur and Mondestin spoke in Creole, fast, trying to decide what to do. The foreigner didn't seem to understand their talk or their worry. He was looking around the beach, planning his pictures.

Paulie felt Adeline stiffen beside her every time the man pointed his camera toward Uncle.

Mondestin warned that to let the newsman take their pictures could bring trouble. "Remember Ti Pierre, Armelle's boy?" he said in a low voice. "*Jounalis* asked him did he want Titid back. All he said was yes, that would be the best thing for Haiti. Next day he just disappeared. Armelle hasn't seen him since." No one answered; Mondestin pulled his Marlboro shirt up over his face and peered through a hole in one of the O's. "Like spy I will talk," he muttered.

No one laughed, though some nodded agreement. Mondestin tugged his shirt down and walked off along the beach, keeping his distance.

Sauveur said, "Look. Everything bring trouble these days. Life is trouble. Rocks in the stream don't understand the suffering of rocks in the sun. They never will if we don't tell them. Let's talk to the *jounalis*. Maybe he can show his pictures to Bill Clinton himself. Maybe this will bring back Titid, to start again ending trouble."

Uncle nodded and stepped forward, getting ready to speak.

Adeline suddenly let go of Paulie's hand and stumbled out between the newsman and Uncle, falling on the sand like a mother bird pretending to have a broken wing. Catching herself, begging pardon for the interruption, she gave Uncle a look of warning, a shake of the head.

Paulie tried to see Uncle's face in the shade of his hat, tried to guess what he was thinking. He took his mother's elbow to help her up and to move her out of the way. Then he turned to the newsman again.

More people from Belle Fleuve had gathered. Uncle opened his mouth to speak, and just then Jean-Desir stepped out of the crowd. He slipped between Uncle and the camera.

"O-kay!" he said loudly, in American language. Jean-Desir moved like a performer, like a *houngan* or priest. He rolled his shirt sleeves just so, borrowed

Sauveur's hat, and turned to the camera as if it were a mirror. "You have question, I have answer."

Paulie shifted her feet, braced one foot against the side of her knee, draped an arm around Karyl's neck. Up near the trees, Lucille stood watching, too, her youngest child, Gabriel, clinging tightly to her skirt.

The newsman began asking questions. Jean-Desir translated each one into Creole. While the crowd discussed the question and how to answer it, Jean-Desir listened, arms crossed, and the camera with its red eye looked at him.

"Why are you building this boat?" the newsman asked first.

"Transport," said Jean-Desir. Sauveur laughed nervously, then made his face long and solemn.

"Why do you want to leave Haiti?"

"We do *not* want to leave Haiti."

There was a brief silence. The people on the beach looked back and forth between the foreigner and Jean-Desir.

"Then why do you need this boat?" the newsman asked.

"To seek Life."

The journalist looked confused and a little angry. He sucked his teeth, shifted his camera, bit his lip.

"What do you mean, 'seek Life'? Can't you live in Haiti?"

Jean-Desir took a deep breath, closed his eyes briefly, and translated the question so the others could discuss it. While they talked, Jean-Desir jogged in place, like a boxer preparing to land a good blow.

Echoing what the others on the beach were saying, he answered the journalist's question.

"No, *msye*, mister. We want to live in Haiti, but we cannot. We are starving in Haiti. We seek Life in Haiti, and we find Death."

The journalist raised his eyebrows, which were very black and full. He looked at Jean-Desir with green eyes, and small pink spots appeared high on his cheeks. Paulie wondered if he could feel his skin change color so.

It seemed to her that the man was angry with Jean-Desir, with all of them. Either he did not believe that Jean-Desir spoke the truth, or he did not think it was polite to talk about life and death.

The journalist cleared his throat. "I understand that economic conditions are bad here, that you might prefer to work in the United States and take advantage of our welfare system and social services. Is that why you are leaving Haiti? Are you running away from the bad economy?" He looked at them all, making it clear, as it was being translated, that the question was for everyone.

Jean-Desir listened to the older people talking among themselves, then told the newsman what they were saying.

"The answer to your question is no, again," he said, frowning. "We do not run away from the economy. For many years we have bad economy, and always we have preferred to stay here in Haiti. Only now some of us must leave, because here, is only Death for us."

The journalist looked at all of them, put his head to one side, and then asked another question.

"Were things better for you when Father Aristide was in office as President of Haiti?"

There was silence on the beach. No one moved, and the only sound was the soft murmur of the waves washing up on the sand.

Jean-Desir's eyes flickered up to the road, to the fringe of trees. Then he looked back at the camera. He spoke clearly, pitching his words to the microphone. Even before he translated, Paulie guessed part of what he said.

"Things were better for us when Titid was in Haiti, yes. We had hope, and we could work for a life. Things will be better again when Aristide returns. But if we wait here until we are dead, it will be too late for us."

Paulie stared at Jean-Desir. These were not thoughts from the radio. These were thoughts from himself. She admired him entirely, and she squeezed Karyl's shoulder, giving her a little sidelong smile to let her know what a fine brother she had.

Also Paulie saw that Jean-Desir wanted to prove himself to Uncle. Now Uncle would truly mean it when he called him "friend."

Adeline was sitting on the beach. Gabriel had his head on her knee, and was sucking his thumb. Lucille had come close, to hear what her older son was saying.

The newsman wasn't through with his questions.

"Who will be the captain of this boat?" he asked. "Who is responsible?"

Everybody looked every way except at Uncle. Jean-Desir cleared his throat, and Paulie's heart rose up in her mouth.

Sweat was gathering just above Jean-Desir's nose. "The captain is Legba," he said.

Everybody on the beach knew Legba, the *lwa* of the crossroads, the *vodou* spirit who must open barriers and allow passage from one state to another. Everybody except the foreigner, Paulie noticed. He held the camera on his shoulder with one hand and patted his pockets for a pencil.

"Is this Captain Legba here? How do you spell that?"

After they spelled it for him, he smiled and said, "That's all I need, and I thank you."

He pulled a business card from his pocket and gave it to Jean-Desir. "It has been a pleasure talking with you," he said. "Tomorrow at noon, there will be a radio broadcast from the United States. I understand that both our presidents will speak."

When Jean-Desir translated this, a murmur rose among the people on the beach, excitement held inside like sea roar inside a shell.

Paulie saw that the foreigner had a pack of business cards, so she held out her hand. He gave her a card. Paulie stuck it in her pocket. She liked things that were printed.

After that, the newsman walked up and down the beach, filming the boat from all angles, the palm trees, the surf. Karyl danced in front of the camera, making eyes and waving her elbows. She tried to pull Paulie into a dance. But Paulie thought Adeline was right about the camera, that it might have some evil in it. Every time the red eye looked at her, she hid behind a palm tree until it turned another way.

7

Poto Mitan

Next day, when the sun was reaching toward its height over the bare mountain to the south, Uncle and Paulie walked hand in hand up the beach, over rocks and through tall grass to a small house that a fisherman named St. Leger had shared with the schoolteacher, Mèt Sadrak, before Sadrak was taken away. Mèt Sadrak owned the kind of strong radio that received Haitian stations, programs from the Dominican Republic, and even Radio Miami.

"Msye St. Leger will be keeping Mèt Sadrak's radio for him, sure as sunrise," Paulie said.

"Hope nobody told the *macoutes* about it," Uncle said.

They weren't the only ones to have remembered Sadrak's radio: when Paulie and Uncle got to St. Leger's, more than twenty people had already gathered in the yard. It seemed almost like a party. Some had brought clothes to sit on as at outdoor church. Others squatted, balancing on long feet, hands dangling loosely over their knees or spread in gestures as they talked softly. Congo grass grew around the yard, dry and warm in the sun, rustling slightly. The grass and rocks hid the people in St. Leger's yard from passersby on the beach or on the road.

People greeted Uncle with jokes, smiles, hands reaching for his. A woman pulled Paulie onto her lap. As each new person appeared, suddenly parting the grass, everyone talked more softly. Paulie felt a fear grow among them that the section chief and his *macoutes* would come as well. The section chief liked to know everything that went on in Belle Fleuve. He lived only a mile down the road, next to the guardhouse. He had told people that gatherings of more than four people were forbidden. Paulie thought the section chief could take away St. Leger's cow for disobeying, just for having people in his yard like in the old days.

Old St. Leger sat on the step of his house, a tin box on his knees. He opened it slowly, unwrapped from a rag six shiny batteries. He lined them up on the dark floor behind him and put away the tin. Then he reached for the radio, pried open the back, and put in the batteries. He did this with great care, his hands shaking.

Paulie wondered if St. Leger was still strong enough to fish. It took strength to get a boat out over the waves. Then she wondered if Uncle himself would be strong enough to flip *Seek Life* off the palm logs and push her out beyond the breakers. . . .

St. Leger turned on the radio. All conversation in the yard stopped suddenly. The speaker crackled, and the old man turned knobs with a frown on his face. Paulie wanted to grab the radio from him, afraid of missing the broadcast altogether. Uncle crossed his arms and stuck his hands firmly in his armpits. A tired-throat voice came from the radio, in English.

"Bill Clinton!" someone whispered, and other people nodded. No one there could understand the words, but they sat patiently. Then a translator came on. The American President was telling them to stay in Haiti. He said that democracy would be restored, and things in Haiti would get better.

"Does democracy mean Titid? That means Titid will come back?" someone asked.

"If democracy mean the people choose, then the people did choose Titid—"

"Shhh!" came several voices.

Titid's own voice came from the radio.

"*Frè'm, sè'm,* my brothers, my sisters . . ." Everyone leaned toward the radio, alert and silent. They heard President Aristide tell them to have courage, to try to hold strong in Haiti, while he tried, with the

American President, to hold negotiations that would allow him to return to Haiti, to continue his government of social justice, without an invasion.

When music came on the radio again, St. Leger turned the radio off. He put it under his arm and withdrew into the darkness of his house like a hermit crab disappearing inside its shell.

In the yard, people sat still, as if afraid to break a spell. Finally Sauveur's mother, Annie Rose, cleared her throat.

"*Titid sé mesie*," she said with conviction. "Titid is messiah." No one contradicted her.

Slowly, people got up, stuck their heads into the dark cabin to thank St. Leger, stepped carefully away through the grass. In twos and threes, they left in separate directions. They seemed to be carrying precious words in their minds like eggs in a basket, and were careful not to interrupt each other's thoughts. Uncle and Paulie said their good-byes quietly, and walked back over the rocks until they found a sandy place to sit and talk.

"What did Annie Rose mean, '*Titid sé mesie*'? " Paulie asked, heaping sand over her foot.

"What do you think, Paulie?" Uncle asked. "I am wondering about it myself."

Paulie was silent.

Titid sé mesie. Titid, Aristide, is messiah. A messiah? The messiah? Paulie turned these words over in her mind, examining them as she might a fish.

Paulie sometimes went to church with Grann.

When churchgoing people spoke of a messiah, they meant Jesus. She thought of some other words people said Titid had said, when he was a priest preaching on the radio. "Jesus is not one person, far away. Jesus is you, the people. Jesus moves in us all. You are messiahs."

"Uncle, I don't know," said Paulie. "You tell me. Is messiah the same as God?"

"A person isn't God, Paulie. Messiah isn't God exactly, I don't think. Messiah is more like spirit of God, spirit that God sends out. . . . The Jesus you hear about in church, they call him messiah because God sent him to wake people up, to make them notice what's right and what's wrong, what's true in the world. So when Annie Rose called Titid messiah, is maybe for the same reason."

"Titid knows what is true in the world?"

"Titid knows what it is like to be poor and to suffer, and also he studies a lot and knows what people in the world think. So he put together this idea called social justice. . . . You interested, Paulie?"

"Yes, Uncle." She almost said no; the talk was making her excited, angry, and sad, all at once.

"This idea of social justice says every person have a right to live, to eat enough so he don't fall down, to do some hard work and earn his living. And that what he earn be for him and his family, not just for some unknown person that happen to own the place where he work."

"The section chief says Karyl and Jean-Desir's

father can't work his land because he has no paper to say he own it. But all his life he been working that land. . . ."

"This whole business to own land is nonsense to me," said Uncle. "Person born, person die, and the land is there for a long time. Who do you think should be responsible for land, Paulie: the one who takes care of it day to day, year to year, or the one who has money in a bank and a paper saying is all his?"

"The person who works the land going to take better care, I think," said Paulie. She let dry sand run through her fingers, watched it fan out on the breeze.

"The journalist didn't believe us," Paulie added. "He didn't believe we want to stay here. He said we wanted to leave Haiti, to leave this land and go take money from foreigners."

"Looking for money and looking for Life two different things, but some people don't know that."

"Not all the way different, Uncle. Person needs—"

"Money to live, Paulie? Sometimes. That's true."

"Sauveur's ma thinks God sent Titid with the message that social justice more important than money?"

"That is surely part of it, Paulie. Is dangerous to call anybody messiah because it sounds like you think they God—"

"Might give person a swell head."

"Might. But Titid himself says he is not the only

50

one. Everybody can be messiah as much as they want to."

"Us, too?"

"Well, yeah, Paulie. Why not?"

Paulie thought awhile, letting sand run from her fist to the beach. "Jesus got killed."

"That's true, Paulie."

Paulie was quiet, thinking.

Uncle smiled suddenly. "Remember, Paulie, when you were little, how you used to always be playing around my workbench when I was building a coffin?"

"What did I do, Uncle? Tell about me."

"Oh, you were full of Jesus talk. Pick up a wood shaving, hold it in the sun, watch the sun shine through. Sing to it. Powder your face and hair with sawdust till you looked like a ghost. Tell me story from church, 'bout how Jesus' father, no, maybe Jesus' uncle was a carpenter. 'You be Joseph, I'll be Jesus,' you'd say. 'Okay, Jesus,' I'd say. 'Fetch me a hinge, Jesus.' "

Paulie laughed. "That was when I was little. And I didn't really think I *was* Jesus, I mean messiah. . . ."

"Every messiah don't have a white face," said Uncle. "And every messiah don't have to get killed."

Paulie was hugging her knees and staring out to sea, so Uncle went on, talking partly to himself. "The way I am seeing it now, Jesus was just one of those in the messiah business of waking people up. I think if you went back in time to where Jesus was, and you said right to Jesus' face, 'Jesus! Congratulations! You going to be the First and Last Messiah, the Big-Shot Messiah of all time!' I think Jesus going to say to you, '*Get away from me*, Paulie! Don't you go piling up that whole load of responsibility on me alone. I'm just one man in the messiah chain. I'm trying to start something, Paulie, not put a stop to it!' "

Uncle's grin split right across his words as he rose to his feet. Paulie let him pull her up.

"See if we can't find some kind of shellfish or seaweed to make a soup, Paulie, else we won't be carrying no message nowhere."

"I see a jelly!" said Paulie, racing for it.

"You want to make me sick, girl?"

Paulie ran down the beach, and then stopped abruptly.

"What's that floating, Uncle?"

Uncle came up beside her. "Look like a big pole to me."

"What people do with a long straight pole like that?"

"Put up telephone wire, maybe . . . no, too small for that." Paulie looked at him; she wasn't familiar with telephones.

"It look to me like the center pole for a worship house."

"You know, Paulie, I think you right! It might be the *poto mitan* from a worship house. . . ." Uncle was taking off his sandals, peeling off his shirt as he talked.

"The pole the spirits travel through," said Paulie.

Just as Uncle dived into the water, Paulie threw her arms around herself and started jumping up and down with excitement. "A mast for the boat!" she shouted, and then clapped her hand over her own mouth. "A mast for the boat," she whispered.

8

Jean-Desir

Uncle drew a triangle in the sand with his toe. The triangle took in almost all the shade under the palm tree. Even the two short sides were twice as long as Paulie.

"Sew together one strong piece of cloth big enough to cover all this sand," he said.

Paulie laid out all the bags and pieces of blue plastic. She turned them this way and that, not only so they would cover every bit of sand, but also to make them look pleasing, a patchwork of blue and brown.

"Make the edges overlap, Paulie, so the sail will be strong where the pieces join up," said Uncle.

Sauveur leaned against the side of *Seek Life*, his hat pulled low, shielding his eyes, his arms folded, looking out to sea. At his feet were a bucket of paint and a brush, waiting to be used.

"Nobody says this boat have to be perfect, Uncle."

Uncle selected boards to plank the side of the boat, planing and shaping each one with slow gentle care. Curls of sweet-smelling wood fell from under his plane onto the sand. From time to time Sauveur gathered them in his hat, carried them over to where Paulie worked, and dumped them into a burlap bag Uncle had said was too loosely woven to use in the sail. The shavings would start many fires.

Paulie smiled at Sauveur's impatience. Uncle wanted the boat to be as beautiful and strong as he could make it. It wouldn't matter to him how long it took.

Uncle fit a board on snugly, nailed it in place, ran his hand over the smooth joint. One side of the boat was almost covered.

The sun warmed Paulie's back as she worked, adjusting and readjusting the pieces that would make the sail.

Sauveur spoke again. "The boy Jean-Desir . . . do you think he'll be in trouble for talking to that foreigner?"

"He wants to join the *kombit*," said Uncle. Paulie stopped crawling around and sat still to listen.

"He earned a right to join. That was fine talk! Did you know the boy had it in him to talk so straight? And in English!" Sauveur shook his head and whistled admiringly. "You know, Uncle, we'll be needing somebody who can speak English, when we get to Mee-ya-mee."

Uncle looked up from his plane. "I say we tell him yes, he can be in the association, the *kombit*. And maybe even be one of the ones to go in the boat. But everybody must agree together on who goes."

"True. And the boat is not big." Sauveur took off his hat, wiped the sweat off the short bristle growing on his head, replaced the hat. "And some people have given materials for the boat. Is not talk alone will get us to the U.S.A."

"What we need next will be tar, Sauveur."

"You know who have all the tar."

Uncle looked at Sauveur, his nose beginning to twitch into a laugh. "Well now, let me see . . . ," he said, putting his head on one side. "Tar."

"Black stuff, to put on the road," said Sauveur.

"Something the government provide for the people," said Uncle.

"Who's that again?" Sauveur asked. "The government? The people? If it for the people, there is only one place it will be."

Uncle nodded slowly, chewing his lip.

"I dreamed I saw barrels of tar up on the section chief's porch," said Sauveur in a whisper, his eyes half-shut.

"Veranda," Uncle corrected, also in a whisper.

"*Grandon* chief has veranda now. *Macoutes* sitting right *on* those barrels of tar."

"Yeah," said Sauveur. "Sitting on the barrels so they don't dance away, drinking *kleren*, slapping domino. Waiting until somebody wants tar bad enough to give them something." He shook his head, sighed, and stood very still. "Only thing we got worth trading be Sadrak's radio, and that belongs to Sadrak, so we can't trade without him here."

"I don't know," said Uncle. "Sadrak was always with us in this project, and this boat is maybe not going to float unless we can tar the seams."

"I think St. Leger would agree to the trade . . . Sadrak, too, if ever he comes back. But who going to make the deal?" asked Sauveur, half to himself. "Maybe Jean-Desir; he does get along okay with those *sans-mamans*." Sauveur frowned at his feet. "But even if he can get tar, as soon as the *macoutes* know we ready to put tar on the boat, they will try to steal it."

"But you know, Sauveur," said Uncle, dropping his voice and raising his eyebrows, "they will wait until we do all the work. That's why we do the finishing in secret. While they waiting for every last bit of the work to be done, we take off."

Sauveur looked at Uncle, his head on one side. "You got it planned, Uncle?"

"Yeah," Uncle said. "I got it planned. Let me send Paulie see if she can find Jean-Desir." Uncle turned to call her. "Paulie!"

"What do you need, Uncle dear?" Paulie asked.

Uncle raised an eyebrow. "You can run an errand for me, take a message?"

"Yes, Uncle."

"Is that we need some tar for *Seek Life*. And the only people who have tar are the soldiers, and we need Jean-Desir to talk to them for us. So I'm asking, can you go find Jean-Desir and tell him come here?"

Uncle looked at his niece, who was looking at him, her jaw to one side. The smile Uncle had been missing lit Paulie's face. "That means Jean-Desir can be in the *kombit*, right, Uncle?"

"Yeah." He nodded. "That's right, Paulie. If the man can only get us some tar."

*P*aulie ran down the road, jumping to touch branches that hung low. Jean-Desir would be on Uncle's side now, with the *kombit*. Uncle was a good judge of people. He believed in the smart, proud boy she had seen on the beach, not in the nervous, shifty boy they saw with the soldiers. And if later on she did go to Mee-ya-mee, and Jean-Desir was there, then maybe Karyl could come, too, and it would be almost like home. . . .

She went to Karyl's *lakou*.

Karyl and her mother, Lucille, were gutting a fish. Gabriel was banging a palm tree with a gong he had made out of a tin can.

"Welcome, welcome. You come to help?" asked Karyl, wiggling bloody fingers at Paulie.

"Uncle sent me to look for Jean-Desir," said Paulie.

58

"Aw," said Karyl. "I think you sent your own self."

"Jean-Desir is working down at tire repair, by the road," Lucille broke in. "He be glad for your company."

"Oh, yes indeed." Karyl crossed her eyes and laughed. "Jean-Desir is pining for your company, Paulie!"

*T*he tire repair shop was an open shed with a firebox inside, and a tub of water, and a high workbench across one side. On the bench were the repair tools shared by all the boys who did this work: a broken clothes iron, a hammer, a pry bar, a glass jar of precious kerosene. Here and there, stuck in the palm-thatch roof, there were bits of foil from cigarette or gum packs, and scrap rubber. Whenever Paulie or any of the other children found these things, rubber or foil, they would bring them to the shed and store them in the thatch.

Jean-Desir was wearing an old T-shirt, his good shirt hanging neatly in a tree. Frail and elderly St. Leger sat patiently on a stump while Jean-Desir dunked his bicycle tire into the tub of water to find where the leak was.

Paulie greeted Jean-Desir and the old man, and then sat beside St. Leger. "I miss Mèt Sadrak," she told him. "If you see Mèt Sadrak, tell him we are always thinking about him and not forgetting the four times seven."

St. Leger smiled, his face stretched up toward the

treetop. Paulie could see the sky and palm fronds reflected in his clouded eyes. He found her hand and bent toward her, whispering loudly. "Mèt Sadrak, he misses you, too. You be one of those he does count on to keep thinking. . . . And something more important than the four times seven." Paulie was not sure what the old man meant, but she heard a step and put her hand over his to get his attention. "Shhh, now, Papa St. Leger. Someone is coming," she warned.

A soldier swaggered toward them on the road, carrying a motorcycle tire. They were all silent except for short greetings. The soldier threw the tire down on the workbench.

"Fix it," he said.

"I get to it right away," said Jean-Desir.

"Fix it *now*," said the soldier. "*Vit-vit-vit!*" He snapped his fingers.

Jean-Desir straightened up and looked at the soldier. He smiled in a friendly way. "This man is waiting already. I'm just about finished with his tire."

The soldier bent over, lifted the bicycle tire from the tub, and threw it in the sand outside of the shed.

He hefted his own *moto* tire into the tub. "This one first," he said.

Jean-Desir's eyes flicked to Paulie and back to the soldier. Paulie wished she were not there. She wanted Jean-Desir to stand up to the soldier, but she wanted him to be safe, too. She turned away, went and got the bicycle tire, brushed it off, and set it against the side of the shed, to have something to do, and to show respect for Msye St. Leger.

She was surprised to turn and see Jean-Desir holding the soldier's tire, dripping wet. He set it against the wall, saying casually to the soldier, "Sorry, Captain. First come, first served. Yours will be ready very soon." He took up St. Leger's tire, put it in the tub of water, and began again checking for leaks. Paulie helped him, leaning over the tub, looking until she saw the little beads of bubbles that led to a hole. "There," she said, holding her finger on the spot until Jean-Desir could mark it.

When she looked up again, the soldier had gone.

She stayed until Jean-Desir finished patching the hole, stuffing it with old rubber, melting the rubber through a piece of foil under the iron heated by a tiny splash of blazing kerosene.

"Uncle sent me to find you. He says can you come talk to him on the beach. They are working on the boat, about ready to do the last seams."

Jean-Desir took off his T-shirt. He put an old cloth in the water tub, wrung it out, and washed. Then he put on his button shirt. Paulie watched, then grinned at him, shaking her head. "You are *so* cool, Jean-Desir!"

The way he walked down the path, she knew he felt good.

9

Moto

Uncle and Grann came home through the trees just as the insects began humming their loud good-bye to light. Paulie was dreaming on the step of Grann's cabin.

"The fire needs building, Paulie."

Adeline's voice startled her, and she noticed it was almost dark. Paulie stood, a little dizzy, and went to find something dry to burn.

As she fed wood shavings to the flames, she thought how she and Karyl could help the men on the beach tomorrow. They could make the fire to keep the tar soft, and mix in the pig hair.

Grann and Uncle showed her tiny black mussels they had found clinging to the rocks. They dropped them in water to boil for a soup. Adeline put in a pinch of salt and a handful of rice grains. They sat together quietly, watching the pot bubble.

"Jean-Desir did bring the tar?" Paulie asked Uncle, softly.

"Yeah, Paulie. The boy did well," said Uncle. "He brought us a whole bucket of tar for *Seek Life*."

Paulie lowered her head, hiding a smile. She had known he would. She had been sure Jean-Desir would find a way to get what the *kombit* needed.

Paulie could smell the rice close to ready, and got their bowls from the house.

When they had eaten, Uncle went to the shed where he did his woodworking. Against one wall stood the cabinet he had built for his tools. Uncle began to unscrew the hinges that held its door in place.

Paulie watched in silence, too tired to ask for an explanation. Uncle brought the door, hinges still attached, over to the fire. Carefully he put the screws he had taken from the cabinet into a cup, which he handed to Paulie.

"Keep these in a safe place."

With a piece of burnt wood from last night's fire, Uncle drew a shape on the door that was like half a gourd.

"The rudder for *Seek Life*!" Paulie exclaimed suddenly.

"Good thinking, girl," Uncle said.

"Good thinking, Uncle," said Paulie. Without being asked, she went and fetched his small-work saw.

A clack of metal and a small thump made them both frown toward the path. Paulie couldn't see anybody in the shadows, but Uncle put his hand on her shoulder and she kept quiet. From the road they heard the *macoute*'s motorcycle sputtering to life.

The roar grew fainter, and Uncle's face relaxed. "They going the right way, for once," he said.

*L*ater, much later, when the moon was high and white, Paulie woke to shouts, a scuffle, and soft thudding of footsteps running outside.

She sat bolt upright on the cot. She heard the roar of the motorcycle, sounding burdened, and rough laughing and shouts. A scream cut the night, drowned suddenly by engine sounds.

"Uncle?" she said, and, sliding to the floor, ran to the corner where he unrolled his sleeping mat at night. He wasn't there.

"Grann!" Paulie knew she shouldn't wake Grann, but she was too frightened to care. Grann didn't wake, but her warm skin and familiar gentle snoring gave Paulie courage. She wiggled into her dress, crept to the doorway, and stopped, staring into the darkness. A man was moving toward her through the trees, running quietly as a shadow. Paulie froze in the moonlight and held her breath. Her heart refused to be quiet and beat loud as a *petro* drum calling the spirits.

He ran bent over, and when he raised his face, looking toward the cabin, it shone wet in the moonlight.

"Uncle!" Relief swept over Paulie so hard she swayed and caught herself on the door ledge. She ran down to Uncle, and he fell on his knees and hugged her to him. She could feel his heart thudding, his breath ragged and confused. Her arms around him, her chin resting on his head, she patted his back, feeling old like a mama, like a tree.

"What happened, Uncle?" she asked.

Uncle spoke in a very low whisper, almost a growl. "Come inside and I tell you."

Sitting on the cot inside, Uncle mopped his face with a shirt. "Look here, Paulie. They took Jean-Desir. They pretended they were taking him to a party. They beat him up and tied him behind the *moto* and drag him up and down the road. . . ."

Uncle put the shirt against his face and rocked, his back shining in the light from the door. Paulie watched him carefully, not letting herself understand his words, holding them away in a corner of her mind, seeing the shapes and shadows of Uncle's back and arm and bent neck.

"Jean-Desir is dead, Paulie. They threw his body on the roadside."

"Wh—"

"They wouldn't let me touch it, or carry it to Lucille."

It seemed to Paulie that they would stay this way forever, stuck in this moment. An ocean roar filled her ears. Her head felt heavy as stone. She curled up like a baby and put her head on Uncle's lap. He covered her shoulders with his damp T-shirt and sat staring into the dark, and rocking, her thin shoulder under his hand.

10

Messengers

 "No!" Paulie said loudly, startling herself awake. She swung her legs over the side of the cot and frowned at the doorway. It was near dawn, the gray light just beginning. She pulled her dress on over her head, taking no time for buttons. There was something she had to do, and she had to do it fast, before she had any time to think about it. She slipped out, balancing on the side of the step so it wouldn't creak, jumping down onto the sand. She made her hands into fists, hunched her shoulders high against the early morning damp, and walked down the path toward the road. When she reached the road, she stood trembling. She made her

eyes scan the roadside, up and down, slowly and carefully. Almost at the bend she saw what she was looking for.

Paulie forced one foot in front of the other until she stood beside Jean-Desir's body. Then she squatted down, folded her arms across her knees. Chin on her arms, she stared.

He was twisted. He was dead. He would never be beautiful again. His good shirt was torn and stained with blood and with dirt from the road. His hands were tied by the thumbs behind his back. He had been dumped facedown. This body was not Jean-Desir. It looked like him, but it wasn't him. It was a husk that still had his shape.

Looking at it made her skin sweat cold, made a burning evil taste in her throat. She swallowed the taste and kept looking.

Every part of Paulie's own body hurt for Jean-Desir, from the soles of her feet flat and cold on the road, through the cramped backs of her legs, to the aching sickness in her stomach, to the strange stiffness in her neck that made her feel her head was twisted forward. Little by little, all the hurts spun and hardened into one big sadness. Like when you would see milk wasted and scattered on the ground, but much more sad.

Paulie stood slowly, as if under a huge weight. Stiffly she walked down the road, took the path in under the trees, dragged some palm fronds back to Jean-Desir's body, and covered it as best she could.

A sudden breeze rattled the palms.

She looked around, expecting soldiers, but too sad to be afraid. No one was there.

Jesus got killed. She remembered saying that to Uncle. Two, three days ago. When he had told her that messiahs were people who told the truth.

Jean-Desir had told the truth when he was talking to the newsman. And he had told the truth when he was telling Lucille he wanted to live. And he had told the truth to the soldier when he had him wait his turn. If doing what is fair is telling the truth. Which Paulie thought it was.

Paulie walked home slowly, her feet dragging in the dust.

Seemed like truth was a habit more than anything else. A habit that got you into trouble. Uncle said he thought everybody could be messiahs. Uncle said every messiah didn't have to get killed. Seemed to Paulie that most did.

She ground her teeth together, her jaw on one side. Habits of truth could kill you. Habits of untruth would make you cheap and shifty, kill the person you wanted to be. In spite of the morning coolness, Paulie felt a sweat break out all around her hair.

She jammed her hand in her pocket, felt something, and pulled out the card given to her by the foreign journalist.

*B*ack at Adeline's house, Paulie crawled into bed and pretended to sleep until Uncle and Adeline had gotten up, talked quietly, and gone to Karyl's house to do what they could to help Lucille. Then Paulie slipped out of bed. She got out her school things, her notebook and pencil, and wrote a note to her family.

Grann and Uncle, I gone Port-au-Prince to tell the *jounalis* what happen. I will come back in three days, *si Dye vle*. I took you leaves, Grann. I love you. Paulie.

Adeline did not read. Uncle read only a little. They would take the note to Jean-De—no, to Karyl, or any of the schoolchildren. She drew many lines around the words, and left the note on Grann's cot. She put some of Grann's leaves in her pocket, along with the card that said ANTON BERTIS, RADYO LAMBI FM, PORT-AU-PRINCE. She trailed her hand a second on the inside of the door, gave the post a pat on the way out.

*P*aulie tried not to think how far it was to Port-au-Prince. She might walk all day and not be there by nightfall, and where would she sleep? But how else to get word to the newsman? She wanted that man to believe what Jean-Desir had told him. It probably wouldn't do any good. Maybe even just to try would make the soldiers madder and meaner. But it was the truest and hardest thing she could do for Jean-Desir, and she intended to do it.

Zong kretyen pa coupe bwa, Adeline's gravelly

voice said in her mind. A fingernail doesn't cut wood. Her Grann used that proverb to scold when Paulie did a job halfway, whenever Grann thought she was giving up too easily. No, a fingernail doesn't cut wood. If you want to do something, you just throw your whole body into it and do it. *Ak tou kò.* She had long legs. She walked fast. Once, hearing a motor behind her, she hid behind a rock. The motor belonged to a military Jeep. Mostly, they were the only ones who had gasoline now. She began saying the times-sevens to her footsteps, to pass the hours and because she had promised Mèt Sadrak she would practice.

"**O**h-eh, *kouman ou ye?* How-a you, how-a you?" a sing-sing voice called from behind her, a high, quiet voice that made her heart jump.

Turning, she saw a thin man on a bicycle weaving down the dirt road between ruts, his knees so far out from his body that he reminded her of a spider. The man had a wizened face, dark glasses, a patched cloth hat pulled low, and a big smile. He bumped once more and wobbled to a stop beside her.

"Are you real for true?" Paulie asked, forgetting her manners.

"You think I am Papa Gede himself?"

Paulie nodded, her mouth still open. Everybody said that Papa Gede, spirit of death, of jokes, of sex, could take the form of a spider.

"No, no, no, little girl. Today I am just a country

priest, traveling to Port-au-Prince on my trusty bicycle in the service of the Lord." He lifted up his hat. He stuck out a hand. "Pè Gerard," he said.

Paulie hesitated. A fingernail . . . She took a deep breath, reached out her arm, and shook the leathery hand.

"Can I—may I—ride with you? Can your bicycle carry us both?"

The man looked his bicycle up and down as if seeing it for the first time. "Rusty bike, trusty bike . . . ," he muttered, and addressed its tires: "Tires! Be strong!" Then he turned to Paulie. "Handlebars or bookrack?"

Paulie, amazed at her audacity, sat sideways on the bookrack, and clasped her hands around Pè Gerard's waist.

"**S**o," said Pè Gerard, "we pass the time with stories, not so?"

"*Cric*," Paulie said.

"*Crac*," said Gerard.

"You," Paulie said.

"Hmm," said Gerard.

"Ti Malis, the Spider, was very, very small. You know that. Ti Malis so tiny he live behind the cross in the graveyard for—oh—one thousand, two thousand year, and nobody even know he there. Although he eat from the spirit feast spread by the cross. He decorate his little corner with the flower petals people bring to put on the graves. He love the song and dance that go along with every *seremoni*.

"Nice thing about being so small is, nobody ever ask Ti Malis for nothing. Nobody say come help me pull all this manioc out me field. No. They get somebody strong for that.

"Nobody say, I got a stump to get out the ground. Come over here, Ti Malis, and grab hold of this rope. No. They call a horse, or maybe somebody corpulent like Bouki, somebody got some weight to him.

"Now, I been talking about what is nice about being small. What is convenient. But one day Ti Malis wake up and he tired of being small. He tired of living off the edges of things, of tricking and stealing. He tired of being a small, small nuisance. After all, Ti Malis very, very clever, not so?

"So what he gonna do? Eh, Lady-Paule? What a small, small spider with big ambition gonna do?"

"Make a web and climb up it?"

"*Enh-HENH!*" said Pè Gerard.

"Ti Malis ate a rose petal here, a chrysanthemum there. Drank some strong rum somebody leave for spirit. A grain of dry corn here, a pinch of white flour from a *vèvè*. Ti Malis sit in his corner and dream his dream of shapes and lines, his dream of good and bad. He churn all this together with a good deal of worry. Then he take a deep breath and he climb skitter-skatter to the top of the cross in the graveyard. He attach the little silk he pull from his own self, and he jump."

Pè Gerard breathed in sharply, then let out a long whistle.

"Ti Malis *fly* through the blue sky. He think, For sure for true, I dead now. I go squash flat on the ground like somebody spit me out.

"But no! The web catch! Ti Malis, he climb up it and attach another piece. For years and years he work so, untangling here, spacing there, making this big beautiful design between the sky and the earth, all around the arms of the cross."

"Ooooh . . . ," said Paulie. Then she asked, "Did anybody else ever see it? Did anybody ever appreciate the web?"

"Not most of the time, no," said Pè Gerard. "That don't matter, though." He pedaled along a smooth stretch, his nose in the air. Paulie craned around sideways to see his expression. His eyes were half-closed behind his glasses and he looked content.

"Only just every once in a while, when the sun catch it just right, somebody notice," he added. "Somebody see how beautiful it is and take heart. . . ."

"*Cric*," said Paulie, clutching Pè Gerard's waist to go over a bump.

"*Crac*," said the priest.

"**B**A-lan-se, BA-lan-se," Pè Gerard urged, leaning the bike heavily first to one side, then the other. "Is stillness stoppers the soul. Throw your body! *AK tou kò, AK tou kò!*"

Paulie, afraid of falling backward, resisted at first, always counterbalancing the priest.

"No!" he shouted over his shoulder. "No no no no no. Push into it! Swoop like a bird. Biggest thing can happen is a life/death shake-up. *BA-lan-se! BA-lan-se!*" he sang, in waltz time.

When she caught on to the swooping motion, Paulie laughed out loud. The frail bicycle looped its way up a long hill in crazy zigzags of energy.

"Be ready, Port-au-Prince! We come! We arrive!" shouted Pè Gerard.

Cresting the hill, they ran smack into an army Jeep and fell over.

*P*aulie picked herself up carefully, aware that many soldiers' eyes were on her. She smoothed down her skirt. *Look sick*, an almost silent voice whispered. She locked all laughter in, pulled sorrow from her chest, nursed it, curled around it. She let tiredness overtake her limbs so that they shook.

"Papers!" one of the soldiers demanded.

Pè Gerard pulled a worn paper from his pocket, unfolding it carefully with the trembling hands of a feeble old man, presenting it upside down. "My granddaughter here, she very sick. She suffers from, you know . . . ," he whispered, "SIDA, AIDS, very bad. I take her to the sisters in Po' Prins. Maybe they can do somethin'. . . ."

Paulie found that her face was hanging slack, tilted to one side. She crossed her eyes slightly, watching the soldiers out of focus, feeling queasy.

"*Woy!* Go, old man!"

Paulie started. The soldiers were waving them on vigorously.

Pè Gerard slowly bent and picked up his bicycle. He pushed it along, one wheel half-turned so that it scraped awkwardly. Paulie limped behind him until the soldiers were out of hearing.

"*Ooooo-eeeee!*" yelled Pè Gerard, so lithe he could have pedaled his bike up a spiderweb. "Get on, La-dy-Paule!"

Paulie wriggled like a chameleon, freeing herself of the protective coloring she had borrowed from a sister she didn't know, grateful to that sick sister. She shook herself up to her full height and climbed on the handlebars.

11

Radyo Lambi *FM*

 Midafternoon in Port-au-Prince, hot and dusty, loud with shouts, motors, and radio music. A smell of diesel and garbage in the air. Pè Gerard rattled his bike down the street, dodging cars and loaded carts, *madansaras* whose wares were spread into the road, schoolchildren in uniform, street children in T-shirts full of holes.

He swooped to a stop in front of a building behind a tall metal fence.

"*Radyo Lambi* FM!" Pè Gerard announced. "Mis Lady-Paule, you have arrived!"

Paulie jumped off the handlebars, brushed her skirt down, turned to say good-bye to Pè Gerard. He wasn't there. She caught a glimpse of him, far down the street, his hat raised in a jaunty wave, pedaling speedily. A car screeched, avoiding him; then he was gone.

So this was the city! Paulie stared. People all around, each busy with his or her life. She did not know even one of these people. For true, she was in Port-au-Prince, and all alone.

Paulie shut her eyes tight and opened them again. The scene was just the same.

The walls of the radio station were pocked with bullet holes. A new metal gate loomed above her, with a small security window, tight shut, just above her head. There was a black button on the wall. A sign above it said RING. Paulie looked at it, thought about it, then carefully pushed the button. Inside the gate she heard an electric noise. She stopped pushing and the noise stopped. Paulie felt her eyebrows go up in surprise. She punched the button once again, fast, and heard another quick buzzing sound. Paulie put her hands behind her back.

Then she heard footsteps inside the gate. The peephole window opened halfway, and eyes blinked out at her.

"What do you want?"

"Ehh . . ." She craned her neck to see into the window. She had not planned what to say. She licked the dust off her lips and tried again. "I bring message for Msye Bertis. Important, yes? Is—"

The eyes turned away, the security window clanked shut. She heard footsteps going inside the building, heard voices. For a moment all was quiet, and she turned her head sideways to see if she could peek through a crack. She heard more footsteps, the window opened, different eyes looked out. Green eyes.

"You have a message for Anton Bertis?"

"Oh! You are Msye Bertis?!"

"You know me?"

"I think . . . I bring message from people in Belle Fleuve. You are the *jounalis* who was in Belle Fleuve, on the beach?"

Two men with guns stuck in their belts walked together down the sidewalk, stopping just beside Paulie. Her voice faltered. She waited for them to move on. They sauntered down the sidewalk a few yards, then stopped.

"Let the kid in," she heard someone say inside. The metal gate swung open just enough to let her through.

Was it the same foreigner who had been on the beach? Did all foreign men have black beards? He led her up some stairs to a bare office and pulled a metal chair toward the desk.

"*Chita*," he said. "Sit."

Paulie sat. The chair felt cold. If she were a dog, he might think to bring her water.

She hoped he would be like a teacher and ask her questions.

"You were one of the children on the beach," said Anton Bertis. "You were afraid of me, no?"

Paulie narrowed her eyes at him. He talked in

79

Creole, but with different sounds from what she was used to. If she stretched her mind very wide, she could understand.

"I only feared the camera," said Paulie. She sat straight and raised her chin. Adeline had been right, too, to tell her stay away from the camera. "You pretended not to talk Creole. . . ."

"We needed English for the camera," said Bertis.

Paulie nodded, staring at him.

"Why did you come here?" Anton Bertis looked at a watch on his arm.

Paulie took a deep breath. Here was her chance to talk. She felt dizzy with it and had to push words out of her throat.

"You did not believe us." She caught her breath, went on fast. "You did not believe Jean-Desir. He said to you we do not want to leave Haiti on the boat. That is true. We do not want to leave. We are forced to leave. People kill us when we try to live as people should. People kill us when we try to be fair.

"Jean-Desir, he tried to tell you. You thought all he wanted was money. He talked to you. He tried to be fair. He fixed Msye St. Leger's tire first and the soldiers killed him and now he is dead. . . ."

Paulie realized that she had risen to her feet, that tears were streaming down her face, that once started she could not stop talking. Her head felt tight and far away from her body. A voice seemed to be shouting higher and higher, echoing around the room. "Uncle says everybody can be messiah, everybody, and sometimes not be killed, even me and Jean-Desir, too, and—"

Anton Bertis was on his feet, holding Paulie by the shoulders. The voice stopped. Paulie felt calmed by his hands, and even though she didn't like him and was afraid of him, she was glad he was helping her stop talking and crying like a crazy person. She heard him call to someone who was in the hall. She heard him say, "I don't know. Damn! Search me. . . . I don't even know who she is. Here. Go get an ice cream. No, get three. Doesn't anybody have a handkerchief?"

The foreigner's voice was so desperate, and what he was saying in his bad Creole was so unexpected, that part of Paulie's sobbing turned into a laugh. She sat down, bent deep over her folded arms, rocking the way Uncle had rocked.

Anton Bertis took her down the hall to a washroom where water came out of a silver pipe into a stained porcelain bowl, and gave her a towel to wash her face, and left her alone while he waited outside.

Paper handkerchiefs were found and put to use. Ice cream was brought. Paulie and Bertis and the gate guard each slowly and solemnly licked away all the sweet coldness and chewed up the cones.

Anton Bertis took a big breath and said, "Now."

Paulie looked up. She felt washed out, empty and clean as a shell.

"Now. I would like to hear everything again,

slow-slow, because your Creole is hard for me to understand, and I will need to translate it into English. And I would like your permission to make a tape recording of everything that you tell me."

"*Eh byen, wi,*" said Paulie. "Yes."

The man turned on a machine on the desk. Paulie told the whole story again. When she came to the part where she had begun the day, the part where she went to see and to cover Jean-Desir's body, she saw that Bertis had his head in his hands. She knew by the shape of his back that he hurt, that he was sad.

When she had told all she could remember, she was quiet. Except for the sounds from the street, the room was quiet, too.

Anton Bertis raised his head. He bit his lip and looked at her with his strange green eyes, and Paulie thought he was trying to decide about something. Then he spoke slowly and carefully.

"Tomorrow or the next day, I will fly on an airplane to Miami, U.S.A. I work for a radio station there. If I could get you a ticket, would you want to come with me and tell your story?"

"No, thank you," said Paulie, without hesitation. "Please, I want to go home."

Anton Bertis looked at her, nodded, and pulled a new little card from a drawer in his desk. He showed her numbers on it. "This is my telephone number in Miami, in case . . ." He didn't finish, just looked at her. "Wait here," he said. "I'll see if I can use the car."

*P*aulie waited, alone, listening to the city sounds. Even a city napped a little, in the heat of the late afternoon, its sounds mixed together into a sleepy drone.

A rattling at the gate below broke the quiet; then a bossy, insistent pounding. Paulie rose to her feet. Before she could move to the door, there were footsteps on the stair, the heavy tread of boots. The door to the office was kicked open.

The two men she'd seen loitering outside the building stood in the doorway. They had brought two soldiers. One of the men swept the tape recorder off the desk. It crashed onto the floor; a piece of black plastic flew across the room. The tape, exposed, wound itself out uselessly. Another man leaned over, hooked a finger in a loop of tape, and pulled out yards of it, stuffing it in his pocket.

Then they turned to Paulie.

12

Garbage

"Come with us."

"Where you gonna take her?"

"To the station."

"Police, or FRAPH?"

"FRAPH."

"A little girl like that . . . Let *me* take her."

The men pushed at her and one pulled her hands behind her back. Another seemed to want to protect her. He wore dark glasses, so she couldn't see his eyes, and held her tight by the elbow, guiding, pushing her down the corridor. Could she trust anybody? Where was Anton Bertis?

The gatekeeper was gone from the hall downstairs. They came out onto the street, and still Paulie did not see Anton Bertis or any other person who would help her. A woman selling pots and pans on the street corner gave her a troubled stare. Paulie was about to call out to her, but the woman looked deliberately away and Paulie thought she did not want to be endangered.

The men pushed Paulie down the sidewalk, around a pile of trash, and over a stream of dirty water that leaked out from an alley.

Suddenly there was a crashing din behind them: the woman had dropped a whole shelf full of tin pots and they rolled on the street. For one moment, all the *macoutes'* heads turned that way. Paulie, remembering games with Karyl and Jean-Desir, twisted loose from the *macoute's* grasp, darted down the alley, took a turn between two shacks, and dived into the first hole she saw.

*I*t seemed to Paulie that nothing in the world would ever make her come out from under that tumbledown, crushed-down house. Flat on her belly like a snake, pressed against some piece of concrete on one side and moldy cardboard on the other, she lay with her face on her elbows, her forearms bent back so that her hands crossed over the back of her neck. She stayed that way a long time, until her eyes lost their stark dryness and began to hurt from her elbows digging into them. The sharp smell of rotting orange peels had become a taste in the back of her throat. When she tried to straighten her arms, they were asleep. Then she became aware of gnawing sounds around her, of furtive scurryings. She realized that there were rats in this place, and without even thinking she began wriggling backward, out of the hole, never mind how dirty and how scared she was. She needed to stand up, and she needed to breathe.

To her surprise, it was almost night. The air was soft and dark and seemed fresh and beautiful now, after the stench she had been in. It angered Paulie to be so dirty. She did not like herself dirty and smelly, and she had to remind herself that it was not her fault. She brushed her dress and spat on the sash and tried to wash her face with it. She pulled at her braids, felt for bits of trash, and pulled them out of her hair.

Two children crossing the end of the alley stopped and looked at her. The smaller one wore only a bracelet of pink beads. Paulie was about to say something to them, but they wrinkled their noses and hurried away. Paulie jumped to dodge a panful of dirty water flung from a doorway. She wondered where to go. She would not go back in the hole to sleep. She had heard that women who came in from the country to sell their fruit sometimes slept in the markets, under the stalls. If she could find a market . . .

Paulie walked down the street, glad that the streetlights didn't work. A few people, sitting on chairs tilted back against their houses, had small lanterns, or tin cans with wicks lit, or candles. These little clusters of flickering light made the street seem darker, and Paulie walked very carefully so as not to fall into one of the many holes that pitted the sidewalk, not to step in the piles of garbage. From time to time, a car passed, with headlights so bright it made the lanterns look dim as shadows. After each car, Paulie stopped walking until she could see again.

A car came, its lights full upon her. She hesitated on the sidewalk, waiting for it to pass. It stopped. Paulie tried to move out of the glare, which would let everyone see her, which hurt her eyes, but for a moment she could not think which way to go and froze there. The car door opened.

"Paulie!"

Who knew her here? Whose voice was that?

"Quick, Paulie, get in the car! Where did you go? Are you hurt? They said they didn't have you, that you'd been released. . . ."

She could see the shape of a man in front of the light. She could see he had a beard. Paulie wondered if she was dreaming, if the whole day had been a dream. She climbed in the car, and before she could answer even one of Anton Bertis's questions, she was asleep.

13

Belle Fleuve

 A jolt tossed Paulie like a rag, and her eyes flew open. The side of her face struck warm, rough cloth. Motor noises growled all around her. She saw lights shining ahead into darkness, making it solid and closed.

The understanding came to her that she was traveling inside a car, at night, bouncing with great speed and violence over a road full of bumps. She sat all the way up, lifting her head from the seat back. Her head felt wobbly, as if her neck were too thin to hold it firmly. The foreign journalist was driving. There was no one else in the car.

Anton Bertis took his eyes off the road to look

at her. The car swerved, caught in a rut. Looking quickly ahead again into the night, he asked how she had slept, shouting because the car noises were so loud. Paulie didn't answer. Her mind was too full of surprise to talk. The car jounced and swayed. They were traveling up a stream bed full of rocks, and she remembered that it was part of the road shared with a stream in the rains. She had bounced down it, on the bookrack of a rusty bike, hanging on to Pè Gerard. Thinking of Pè Gerard made his voice come right out of her throat.

"*BA-lan-se!*" it whispered.

Paulie relaxed suddenly, her anxiety gone. She had done what needed to be done, had thrown herself into it *ak tou kò*. Now she was headed home, bringing the newsman with her.

"What did you say?" shouted Bertis.

"*BA-lan-se,*" Paulie whispered softly. And then, louder: "*BA-lan-se, BA-lan-se!*" She made sweeping gestures with her shoulders, shifting to the edge of the car seat, dancing with the motions of the ride.

Bertis laughed.

"I smell," Paulie shouted.

"True," Bertis shouted back. "You hid in garbage."

"True," said Paulie.

"We're going home?" she asked him.

"Belle Fleuve," said Bertis. He made a gesture as if he were lifting his hat to her, though he wore no hat.

*B*elle Fleuve was dark, and lay in anxious silence. To Paulie, the sound of their car was loud, too loud, even when Anton Bertis rolled as slowly and quietly as he could. Paulie knew how the sound of a strange car coming down the road at night could wake a person and make fear twist in her belly, could make a person hold her breath, wondering what new trouble the car might bring. "Is *me*," she wanted to say. "Is only me, Paulie, coming home." She felt as if she could have grown old or that everyone might have moved away in the time she had been gone.

She slipped from the car at the end of the path to Grann Adeline's house. She ran quickly down the path and up the house steps. She stood in the doorway until her eyes grew accustomed to the blacker darkness inside. Adeline's cot was still made up smoothly. Uncle's mat was rolled in the corner. No Adeline. No Uncle. Disappointment rose in her like a flood.

They're looking for me, Paulie told herself. Slowly, she walked back to where she had left Anton Bertis. Before she got to the end of the path, she heard noises. There was scuffling of feet, heavy breathing punctuated by small thuds. Paulie broke into a run. The car was still there, but Bertis wasn't in it. A little farther down the road, she made out two forms.

Grann Adeline was dancing with the journalist? No.

Grann Adeline was trying to kill the journalist.

They were clutched together, reeling in slow circles.

90

"Grann!" Paulie called softly but urgently. Nobody shouted at night, for fear of bringing the section chief. Adeline's strong old hands were locked around Bertis's neck. A sound like a tire losing air came from one of them.

The hardest thing around is my head, Paulie thought desperately. I will butt them apart. She lowered her head, bracing it into her shoulders. She tried to imagine that she was a truck. As fast as she could run on the dark road, she sped toward them. She raised her head for a split second to make sure her aim was true: the dance in the road stopped as two faces turned toward her. At the moment before collision, the two figures lurched apart. Paulie ran right between them and clutched at air to keep from falling.

"Paulie! My soul!" Grann ran after her, limping, and gathered Paulie to her. "I thought he had killed you!"

She patted Paulie up and down her body, as if to make sure she was all still there, and then suddenly wheeled and ran back to Bertis, who was standing in the road checking his own bruises. He flinched when the old lady darted toward him, but not in time to avoid a loud kiss on the face.

"Tell him," Adeline said to Paulie. "Tell him I won't kill him, since, *Bondye bon*, you are back. But tell him also crabs don't belong in the squash patch. He should quick go home, back where he came from, not to—"

"Grann," Paulie said, "he understands you. He speaks Creole. Just talk slowly." She was a little proud of Bertis now, and didn't want Grann to think he was stupid.

Adeline turned deliberately back to the journalist. She put her hands on his shoulders and her face close to his. "Young man," she said, "Msye Whoever-You-Are"—she shook him vigorously—"Go! Go! Go! My friend Lucille, if she finds you, will kill you even worse than I did."

"Why, Grann?" Paulie asked.

"Because," said Adeline, still speaking to Bertis, "because her son Jean-Desir is the boy who answered your questions. The way Lucille look at it, you killed her boy. And Lucille is a woman used to skinning fish. Little fish, and big fish, too."

For the first time, Paulie noticed that in the darkness Bertis's face looked like the underside of a fish belly.

"Get inside you car, light the motor, plug the spark, do whatever make it run, and go away from Belle Fleuve. *Now!*" Adeline ordered, still staring at Bertis and opening her eyes wide on the last word.

Paulie moved behind Anton Bertis, just to say good-bye. Grann Adeline grabbed her arm, spinning her around. "You stay with me, Paulie. We two, you and me, are going to a wake."

14

Desouni

Paulie followed Grann to Lucille's house, hanging tight to her bony arm, rubbing against her with every step.

"You trying to trip me up, girl?" her grandmother asked.

"Just making sure you really there, Grann."

"I'm here all right. You see me, don't you?"

"No," said Paulie, and giggled. She bumped her hip into her grandmother. "I feel you." Suddenly her tiredness lifted away. The stars were fading, and there was a stirring in the tops of the palms.

"The boy's wake be over soon," said Adeline.

"What will we do for this wake?" Paulie asked.

"Same as always. Watch by the body, pray, sing real soft. Can't beat drum. Can't sing loud to call the spirit, because of the—" She gestured with her chin in the direction of the section chief's house. "But the *houngan* come by already, for the *desouni*. The spirit come separate from the body, so is okay we bury the body now. Your Uncle make a nice coffin for the boy. . . ."

Paulie thought it was a good thing that Jean-Desir's spirit was free from his body now, because he would not like to be ugly or dirty. He would feel shame. She knew his mama and the other ladies would have washed him well, but still, he would never look so very cool again.

She pulled on her Grann's hand. "What will *I* do at the wake?"

Grann said, "Mostly the children just play in *lakou*. Bring rum for the men. Play all those jumping games."

"Okay," said Paulie. "I can play those games."

*T*he night stretched long, a soft dark dampness. People wandered home, until just a few were left at the wake. Word had been sent to Jean-Desir's father, through a man who might know where he was hiding now. Uncle thought it would be many days before word reached him.

Grann stayed inside with Lucille. Once, when Paulie went in to see her, she found both women, each in a chair on either side of the closed coffin, each bent low with her head resting on the coffin. Paulie didn't know if they were praying or sleeping, so she tiptoed out without making a sound.

Mondestin, Sauveur, and Uncle passed a small rum bottle and played cards. Karyl and Paulie let Gabriel play with them. He didn't know his big brother was dead, truly dead forever. Karyl and Paulie made up games Gabriel would like. Sauveur let them build a tower with his dominoes. They took turns putting on a domino, trying not to be the one to make the tower topple. It rose up to Gabriel's head, wobbling. Paulie stood to place her domino on the tower, muttering under her breath, "Wind, don't blow. Earth, don't shake." Then she did feel the earth shake, just a little, and heard a car coming up fast.

The tower fell, Gabriel burst into tears, Karyl grabbed Paulie, the men sprang to their feet. Anton Bertis's car, covered with dust, screeched to a stop beside Lucille's yard. Bertis was out almost before it stopped, looking around him like a wild man. Lucille came to the door, her big knife in her hand. Paulie ran to Uncle, who was approaching Bertis, shaking his head to warn him away. But Bertis spoke to Uncle, and Paulie caught a few words: *section chief, roadblock, guns.*

"They want to stop you, they plan to steal your boat and sell it to someone else. They didn't know I understood what they were saying. They were laughing about exchanging tar for a radio . . . ?"

Uncle stood for a minute staring at Bertis. Staring

through him, Paulie thought, trying to see what he was made of.

Then Uncle asked Bertis a question.

"Can you keep them busy for one hour?"

"Will one hour be enough?"

Neither answered, but Bertis slid back into his car, slammed the door, and was gone in a cloud of dust, lit red by the car's back lights.

*U*ncle waved his arms in a circle that brought them all near. His eyes were weary, his breath smelled of rum, but he looked around the circle of faces, and to Paulie it was like he splashed them with his affection and his calm. All he said was:

"Mondestin, Sauveur, dig the grave for the boy. Lucille will tell you where. Lucille, Adeline, gather belongings. Bring something to make shelter from the sun. Gabriel, Karyl, find any food and jugs of fresh water, many as you can gather. Paulie, go to St. Leger's place. If Sadrak there, see does he want to come. All we meet at the boat soon as we can, to help roll her, step the mast, and push her out."

Then each person turned to do his part.

*S*adrak? Paulie thought. Mèt Sadrak is around here still? He was just hiding, then? Nothing surprised her anymore, but she was glad to know her teacher was alive. She did not think about the sea, or Mee-ya-mee, just about finding Mèt Sadrak.

*I*n the first grayness before dawn, she could barely make out St. Leger's cabin, deep in the grass. She rapped lightly on the door. They were not far from the section chief's house.

Immediately the door opened. Sadrak himself. Paulie, amazed to see her teacher, stood on her toes and kissed him on the cheek, the way students greeted him at school after a break.

"*Respè*, Paulie," he said, smiling, but tense. "Your Uncle sent for me?"

"Yes, Mèt. It's time, and the soldiers are coming."

Sadrak picked up a bundle from his cot. He fell on his knees for a moment beside the other cot, where Paulie could see old St. Leger's knees. He must be sitting there, preparing to rise.

"If you will come, I will carry you," she heard Sadrak say calmly.

"No," said St. Leger. "Bless you."

Paulie turned away with a lump in her throat and stepped down to wait in the yard. When Sadrak came out, he gently closed the door behind him.

*S*till it was barely light. The surf made a white line that undulated like a snake between land and sea, separating and recombining gray from gray to gray. Away to the east the sky was paler, and still the sun kept all color deep in the water.

The surf had its roar, its everyday swishing forward and gurgling retreat, and as Paulie and Sadrak cautiously approached *Seek Life*, they became aware of another sound almost like surf, the breath of people throwing their strength together, counting in whisper: one, two, *threeee*. One, two, *threeee*. Each time, on the count of three, *Seek Life* inched closer to the water. Lucille, Karyl, Adeline, Uncle, Mondestin, Sauveur, even Gabriel—they worked as one, their hands splayed against the newly painted hull like black stars. They didn't break rhythm for Paulie and Sadrak, just moved slightly apart. Paulie slipped in between Sauveur and Adeline, throwing all her weight against the hull on the count of three. The hull smelled of fresh tar, and tar stuck on her hands.

A reaching wave had touched the prow when they heard shots. Still no one broke rhythm. Two pushes later, the boat lightened on a surge of surf.

"Everyone except only Sauveur and me get on board," Uncle said calmly.

"Step in my hands," said Adeline, and boosted Paulie up. In the same movement, Paulie turned, bent from the boat, grasped Gabriel's hand, and hauled him aboard. In that moment, she felt *Seek Life* slip free of the sand and saw Adeline struggling over the stern. When she looked again, surf was breaking all around them, and only Uncle and Sauveur were still in the water. Then their hands grabbed the gunwale; one on each side, balancing each other, they slithered into the boat.

"Keep your heads down," said Uncle. "Bullets flying about." He himself stood to tend the sail. The boat pitched wildly. Paulie lay in the bottom, one arm around Gabriel, Karyl somehow thrown across her legs, every muscle suddenly sore and tired. The wind caught the sail, and the boat steadied. For the second time that night, Paulie passed into a deep sleep.

15

At Sea

Paulie opened her eyes to a bright blue sky. The sail bellied full, carving a crescent of blue between its patchwork and the mast.

All around, framing the blue of the sky, Paulie saw knees. Beyond the knees, faces. Karyl and Gabriel were sprawled across her. All three lay in water. The hard edge of the keel dug into Paulie's back. She picked out Adeline's knee, grasped it, pulled herself to a sitting position. Karyl moaned and curled herself tighter.

"*E lannwit?*" asked Adeline in the morning greeting of Belle Fleuve. "How was the night?"

Paulie rubbed her forehead on Adeline's knees

and squinted up again, her eyes adjusting to the brightness. Grann Adeline squinted at her with sparkling eyes.

"Long," Paulie replied, drawing it out. She crawled up onto the bench that Uncle had built running around the inside of the gunwale. She kissed Adeline on the side of her face, then Lucille, who seemed not to notice. Paulie wedged herself in tightly between them. The brightness on the water astounded her, and the fresh breeze. They were moving fast.

Behind the gurgling wake of the boat, land rose out of the water, purple and pink and hazy, mountain behind mountain behind mountain.

"*Dèyè mòn gen mòn,*" Paulie whispered. Beyond the mountain, more mountains. It was a proverb she had heard forever, meaning that there was always more work to be done, another effort to be made. But she had never seen all at once how many mountains there were, rising behind Belle Fleuve.

"This way, too," said Adeline, nodding toward the bow. Paulie looked and saw what she meant. One behind the other there were waves and waves and more waves.

"Will there be mountains in Mee-ya-mee, Lucille?" Paulie asked, putting her head on Lucille's shoulder.

Lucille didn't move, didn't speak. Grieving for Jean-Desir, Lucille acted dead herself. Paulie missed the Lucille she knew, with the big voice and strong opinions. Lucille's last argument with Jean-Desir came to her mind, and brought tears suddenly to sting her eyes.

She looked down at Karyl, sleeping uncomfortably in her Sunday dress, her Sunday shoes and white socks. Her head bounced against bare wood when the boat bumped over waves. Adeline unwrapped a cloth from around her waist. Paulie folded it into a pillow and tucked it under Karyl's head.

Gabriel woke, and Adeline took him on her knee. His face was puffy and smeared with tar. He looked solemnly at all the faces in the boat. *"Kote frè'm?"* he asked. "Where's my brother?"

Before anyone could answer, a flock of flying fish came skimming across the water.

"Ooooh!" said Gabriel, following them with his finger. Then he put his finger in his mouth and leaned against Adeline. Lucille kept staring across the waves.

*E*ven through the heat of the day the wind drove them on. A good wind.

"*Seek Life* has taken wing," Uncle declared with satisfaction.

The nine people on board shifted positions, took turns sitting up at the bow, or napping on the bundles on the floor of the boat.

"Whenever you see water creep through down there, you take this cup and bail it out, okay, Paulie?" Uncle was pleased that the seams leaked so little.

They passed around a jug of water, hand to hand, each careful not to take more than needed.

102

Later the men moved forward, pretending to look for islands ahead as they talked, so that the women could wash and relieve themselves. Paulie wiggled quickly out of her dress, which reminded her of the garbage of Port-au-Prince, and into the school clothes Grann pulled from her bundle.

Uncle and Gabriel didn't have hats. Uncle put a wet cloth on his head, knotted in the corners so that it wouldn't blow away. He rigged the same cover for Gabriel.

"You look good, Gabriel," he said, saluting the little boy. Gabriel, sitting on Adeline's lap, stared at Uncle, his thumb in his mouth.

After a lull at sunset, the wind kept steady in the night. The stars were very bright. There was no land anywhere.

Uncle showed Paulie the *Kwi*, the big gourd dipper in the night. Showed her how the two stars in the lip of the *Kwi* point to one bright star by itself, the Pole Star, the North Star.

"We go north by night, then. . . . And by day, Uncle? How do you know how to go in the day? By the sun?"

"By the sun. And I have compass. Don't know if it's reliable, though."

"Let me see," said Sauveur.

"Careful, careful," Uncle cautioned, reaching it out to him. Something very small and round changed hands.

Sauveur looked at it in disgust. "That thing nothing but a toy, Uncle. You must'a win that thing at a priest picnic."

"**C**ric!" Sadrak whispered to Paulie and Karyl, who were sitting beside him in the bow.

"*Crac!*" Paulie and Karyl answered together.

"This one is a true story."

"Okay, Mèt," Paulie said. Any story was fine with her.

"This is a story about finding your way by night, by day, and in the world."

"Tell it, Mèt," said Karyl.

"The story is about some men and women captured by slave traders in Sierra Leone, Africa, in the year 1837," Mèt Sadrak began.

"A history story," said Paulie, pulling Adeline's cloth around Karyl and herself, wrapping them tight together. They were in the nineteen hundreds now, almost the twenty hundreds. But it didn't matter, because she could imagine being forced by her elbow down a path, held the way the men in the radio station had held her. She could imagine being tied and thrown into a boat.

"Men and women, captured as they go about their lives in Africa, are stripped of their clothes, thrown naked in the belly of a ship," said Sadrak. "Chained together by their legs. Dirty in there, in the hold of the ship. Not much air. The men and women of Africa must struggle to keep their dignity, guard each other's privacy. They turn away from the body misery that does not want to be witnessed. They only look each other in the eye. They talk. They plan.

"Finally the big ship touches the island of Cuba. Some of the men and women are sold there, to a big sugar plantation. The others watch, listen, learn what is in store for them. The ship they call *Amistad* sets sail for the other end of the island of Cuba. The men and women of Africa know they will be sold there, sold and separated. They develop a code: three jerks on the chain mean is time to act. They watch for opportunity. One day they distract the guard, causing him to forget to lock their chain after exercise. They rise together, break loose, chain the captain, take the ship."

"Good for them," Karyl said, hugging Paulie. Sadrak closed his eyes, then looked up at the stars and continued.

"Some have been watching how the ship is sailed. Learning by watching, the men and women of Africa have prepared themselves. They are capable of sailing the ship, and they do.

"All night, they sail by the stars. Keep the North Star over your left shoulder, and you heading east. East is Africa. East is home.

"But by daylight, a sailor fools them with false advice. Trying to get back to Cuba, to win reward, he persuades them to turn the boat astray, north instead of east. . . ."

"What happened, Mèt Sadrak?" asked Karyl. "Where did they end up?"

Sadrak smiled, and shook his head. "They came to shore in the U.S.A., in a seaport called New London. People there so surprised to see them! Africans sailing a ship! Some people are riled because they say these Africans *steal* the ship. But many people there against the idea of slavery anyway, and this prove to them again that slavery is pure foolishness, not to mention evil.

"They have the biggest court case ever. *Eh!* You should have heard, Paulie, Karyl. White men in wigs yelling at each other for three years or more."

"What!" both girls asked together. "Why the men wearing wigs?"

"Can't answer that one, daughters, but is true. White men in that time put a sheep wool on their head to look smart."

"How anybody going to look smart with a sheep fur on they head?" asked Karyl. "No way."

Paulie rested her head on Karyl's shoulder. "Then what happened?"

"First the judge says the men and women of Africa steal their own selves away from their rightful owners, and on top of that commit murder, because one of the crewmen did die in the shake-up."

"How can they steal their own selves?" Paulie asked indignantly.

Sadrak laughed. "That's what *they* say, Paulie. Now listen:

"The lawyer for defense say, 'Ah-ah-ah! Wait a minute! If the men and women of Africa be people, can't nobody rightfully own them, except only their own selves. If on the other hand they be in fact *things*, things they call chattels that can be owned, then they can't be held responsible for human crimes like stealing and murder.

"You see, Paulie? You see, Karyl?

"The lawyer for the defense say the judge have to choose. The case sounds simple, but the men in wigs love to argue. They drag it on for a long time."

"And what is happening to the men and women of Africa?"

"Well, Paulie, the men and women of Africa all this time freezing their feet in New London waiting for the judge to decide whether he think they are human or not. But they are not altogether wasting the days. They learning to speak English. They learning to write letters. The men and women of Africa write to the President of the United States. The men and women of Africa get ordinary white people, and people in government, and all kinds of writers and church people on their side. They argue peacefully every step of the way, until finally the judge agrees: yes, okay, the men and women of Africa human people, too. . . ."

"What else he think they gonna be?" Karyl asked the sky. Her face, tight as a fist in the starlight, suddenly looked like her brother's.

"So then the judge charged them with murder and stealing and everybody had to argue about 'just cause' and all that.

"Finally the judge said, *Enough!* To stop all the talk, he allowed some people with money to buy the men and women of Africa passage on a ship and send them back to Sierra Leone."

"Sierra Leone, Africa? For true?" said Paulie.

"For true," said Mèt Sadrak. "And just about twenty years after that, there was a big war between the states, to end slavery forever."

"Did it?" Paulie asked.

"I'm not sure," said Mèt Sadrak.

*M*ondestin pushed his hat to the back of his head. "You ask me, Sadrak, slavery not over."

"The kind of slavery they did have, where the slaver actually protected by the law, that kind over, Mondestin," Sadrak said.

Mondestin shook his head. "It still the same, Sadrak. They just done made it more complicated, so people not get so outrage."

"Pull on that rope, Sadrak," said Uncle. "Sail flapping too much."

"How you see it working now, Mondestin?" Sadrak asked, tightening the rope.

Mondestin was silent a minute. When he spoke, all Paulie could see of him was his long hands gesturing. "Fact is," he said, "if you got some little money, some capital, you can work for yourself. You have a say in your work. If you not have capital, if you can't get capital, then you must work for somebody else."

"Working for somebody else not the same as slavery, Mondestin," said Sadrak.

Mondestin took off his hat, turning it and turning it in his graceful hands. "If I work for somebody else and I get paid, enough to have a house and some food, enough for Life, you know, then that not slavery. . . . Of course not. But who got that situation in Haiti now? Nobody! Almost nobody!

"Because the people that have capital, who buy up the land, who run the big sugar plant or the assembly factory, they can pay anything they want, any little nothing they want, and the person who work all day for that money cannot even live from it himself. And his family going to starve. That's why I say we still have slavery."

"How come they set it up so unfair?" Paulie asked.

"Some countries have a bottom-wage law," said Sadrak. "In those countries, even the person who not paid much can earn enough to live. But in a country that have no bottom-wage law, the rich get more rich, and the poor get more poor. Until the poor man have nothing at all. And when he too weak to work, the boss just throw him out and hire somebody else."

"Paulie, you want to take a turn sleeping now?" Uncle asked. Sauveur had just gotten up, crawled up from the floor to join the conversation. Paulie slid down into the darkness of the hull, between people's feet. Karyl gave her the cloth to pillow her head. Through it she could hear the sloshing of water against the hull. She could feel it the whole length of her body. Paulie breathed in the combination of fresh air and tar and feet, and thought about what the men were saying. She tried to imagine what Uncle called "social justice." She pictured it radiant, the way heaven sounded in church songs. But maybe it just meant a way of setting up jobs so Mondestin and his girlfriend, Mireille, could work and earn enough to have a house and raise children.

She wondered whether she and Uncle and Grann Adeline would have a house in Mee-ya-mee, or whether they would live under the boat.

16
Cutter

Paulie woke sometime before dawn, miserable with needing to pee and too embarrassed to use the tin with everyone so close together. It crossed her mind that if she went very quietly in the bottom of the boat, everyone would think Gabriel had done it. She gazed up at the gray sky and felt sick.

Sadrak and Uncle were talking.

"We haven't seen one cutter," said Uncle, a kind of reverence for their luck in his voice. "Not one."

"*Bondye bon,*" Adeline murmured, her chin on her chest, commenting on the conversation or talking in her sleep.

"One cutter alone would be too many," said Sadrak. "They take us aboard a U.S. Coast Guard cutter and we be right back in Haiti before sunup."

"What would the U.S. Coast Guard people do to us?" Paulie asked from the floor.

"They would take us to the dock at Port-au-Prince and give us over to FRAPH. They would smear ink on our hands and make us leave prints of our fingers on their official papers like we did something wrong. They would ask us where we come from. They would even call the section chief so we be sure to have a reception committee waiting for us in Belle Fleuve."

"Is it true they would . . . ," Uncle began, his voice trailed off, and he curled his fingers around the gunwale.

"Blow up *Seek Life*? That's what I hear, my friend. Everybody says the U.S. Coast Guard blows up Haitian boats and sinks them so nobody can use them again."

Uncle cleared his throat. "They say on the radio our boats nothing but trash."

"Hey, Uncle. Some people say on the radio that *we* are nothing but trash, and look how it is not so. . . ."

Sadrak and Uncle both looked down at Paulie. Here was her chance to tell them her need, but she closed her eyes, mortified.

Just then Sauveur called from the bow.

"Something big floating, Uncle. Careful."

Uncle and Sadrak both stood to look ahead. Paulie

stumbled to her feet. She sat quickly on the bench, her legs wound around each other like squash vines. Out on the gray water she could see trash floating: boards, a few pieces of Styrofoam, some tins.

"Looks like somebody sank a boat, Uncle," said Sadrak. "Looks like maybe the U.S. Coast Guard is near."

Silently Sauveur stood in the bow and pointed.

A huge gray shape loomed on the edge of the waves. It grew soundlessly. A humming came through the boat and traveled up Paulie's legs.

"*Djab!*" said Uncle.

He and Sadrak touched each person's face, shaking them, waking them, urgently pointing out the cutter. Uncle took charge.

"Sauveur, help me bring down the mast. Sadrak, Mondestin, slip over into the sea. Hold on to the boat tight-tight. Do not let go for anything. The lower we are in the water, the less they will see us. Throw over anything metal. Maman, *ti moun*, Lucille: lie flat in the bottom of the boat."

"I'm going, too, Uncle," said Paulie, and before he could stop her she slid over into the waves, hanging on to the gunwale of *Seek Life*. Water closed around her body, warm and welcoming.

"Hold tight, Paulie," said Sadrak anxiously. She saw him fill their metal tin, watched it sink below the surface. Then he slid over the gunwale and was in the water beside her.

"Your Grann, Lucille, and the children are lying

down," he said to her. "All the rest of us will hide in the water."

"Why?" Paulie asked, feeling not afraid but wonderfully relieved.

"The Coast Guard radar machine only picks up what is above the water," said Sadrak.

"And metal," added Mondestin, clinging now on her other side. "Radar picks up metal."

"Drop your belt, then, Mondestin," said Sadrak.

"No way!" Mondestin grimaced, lowering himself in the water so that his belt buckle was well covered.

Uncle was still in the boat. He and Sauveur pulled the sail down hand over hand, throwing it on top of Grann and Lucille, Karyl and Gabriel. They wrestled the mast out of its mount and laid it flat across the boat, where it kept the sail from flapping in the slight breeze. Even from where Paulie clung, *Seek Life* looked suddenly small, like a *kwi* or a nutshell. She put her ear against the boards. She could hear the people inside; Gabriel was crying in a small plaintive voice. Grann was singing softly, trying to quiet him.

"Cina, Cina, Cina"

It was a praise song for the spirit of the sea, for Agwe.

"Agwe Arroyo, care for your little ones . . ."

Paulie had thought that a cutter would have a knife coming out of one side, a long curved knife that would slice across the water.

This cutter was a rectangle of darkness. It got bigger, darker, and the whole sea throbbed around it.

"Seashell in hand, protect your children"

Adeline was still crooning.

It seemed to Paulie that the sea was growling at the cutter.

"Where is the knife?" she whispered to Sadrak.

"There is no knife," he answered, looking at her strangely from the corner of his eye.

Paulie stared at the cutter with absolute concentration. Her arms felt like metal bands. Her toes braced against the bottom of *Seek Life*. They wanted to float to the surface and it took all her strength to keep them down deep.

She could see people moving on the cutter. Music from a radio floated over the water. Something glinted like two tiny moons, high on a sort of walkway, close together. Paulie stared back, not blinking.

"Hold tight!" Sadrak whispered. *Seek Life* rocked suddenly in the wake of the big ship.

Had the cutter grown smaller, paler? Paulie, dizzy, took a deep breath. She closed her eyes tightly, willing the cutter to be gone.

When the sea quit shivering, she opened her eyes.

At that moment, the cutter disappeared and the sky turned from gray to pink.

Paulie's fingers were shriveled; her arms ached. Karyl leaned over the side of *Seek Life*, dabbling her hands in the coolness, splashing her face. Paulie wanted to let go and sink into the vast lovely comfort of the water.

"Can I swim?" she asked Uncle.

"Close by," he said. "Three out, three in."

Paulie was already splashing a waterspout up into the sunrise in the middle of the sea.

After Uncle pulled her back on board, after he and Sauveur had stepped the mast once again and tied the sail back in place, he grinned mischievously and reached deep under the floorboards. He pulled out a large conch shell, with one end cut away. He reached it toward Paulie as he settled at the tiller and found the wind.

"A *lambi*! We brought a *lambi*!"

The wind caught in the sail of *Seek Life* once again. The wake began to gurgle.

"Blow it, girl. Now we are truly on our way."

Paulie curled her fingers inside the pink smoothness of the conch shell and put one end to her mouth, holding it up like a trumpet. Hard as she could, she blew. A loud, wild sound flew from the shell. Karyl stuck her fingers in her ears. Gabriel took his thumb out of his mouth. A laugh spread across his face. He reached out both hands and said, "*Me!*"

17

Guinea

"We moving, Paulie." Sadrak held the tiller lightly. "It might not look like we moving, but we are."

The wind was just enough to fill the sail, but *Seek Life* left less trail than a tree snail, and the gurgling under the boat had quieted. Adeline draped her bedsheet across a pole and tacked it to the gunwale with Uncle's hammer and nails, making a shelter from the sun. Uncle stretched on the floorboards in the half shade, and slept at last.

"How come we moving if we don't look like we moving, Mèt?"

Sadrak laughed. "Sound like you don't believe

me, Paulie. We moving the same way I be telling the truth. Just because it don't appear that way don't mean it not so."

Paulie smiled. Mèt Sadrak liked to talk in riddles. "And how's that?" she asked.

"You know about rivers in the sea? About currents?"

"Current pushing us?"

"A river in the sea, a big deep current called the Gulf Stream, is carrying us north. And since all the water traveling with us, it look like we not even moving."

"And where all that water going to go when we get to Mee-ya-mee?"

"To New London," said Sadrak.

Paulie squinted at him, her head on one side, trying to see if he was serious.

"North toward New London, then out across the ocean to England. We got to get out of this Gulf Stream before too long."

"If we stayed in it, could we go on back to Guinea/Africa?" Paulie asked, suddenly excited. "Why don't we go to Africa instead of Mee-ya-mee?"

Sadrak took his time thinking over the question, and Paulie watched him closely to make sure he didn't drift off from answering. If only she had something she could give him to eat, some melon to cool his throat.

"Is some question, Paulie," he said at last. "Part of the reason is that it is just too far to go to Africa in a boat this size. Another part is that the Gulf Stream does not run clear to Africa. But that is not the whole answer, the truest answer. . . ."

Paulie waited, watching Sadrak think.

"The whole more honest answer have to do with Guinea/Africa herself, what Guinea/Africa is for the children of the children of the men and women who were taken from Africa long ago."

"For us," said Paulie. "Me and Gabriel and Karyl and all we. . . ."

Sadrak nodded.

"To us, Guinea/Africa is not a place anymore." Sadrak tapped his foot against the floorboards of the boat, a worried expression on his face. "The land of Africa is there. We could go to it, we could walk the beaches, climb the mountains, wade in the rivers. Maybe we would feel that we had come home. . . . But maybe, Paulie, we would not feel that way. Africa, the land of Africa, could be a strange land to us.

"But that is not true of Guinea/Africa. Guinea/Africa is not a place like that. Guinea/Africa is true home, because Guinea/Africa is a way to be. It is more understanding than place. It did begin with us in Africa, but it has been shaped by every day that the men and women of Africa, and their children, and their children's children have lived."

"You saying that Guinea/Africa is us?"

Sadrak shifted the tiller gently back and forth, trying to push them along, thinking.

"Us, yeah. But that is too simple, Paulie. We touch on it sometimes. . . ."

"When Grann talks to crabs."

Sadrak looked puzzled.

"Or—music?"

"Mostly just living," said Sadrak.

Paulie had a sudden vivid picture of Jean-Desir, looking up from the tub of water where he checked tires for leaks, saying to the soldier, "This man is waiting already. I'm just about finished with his tire."

"So Guinea/Africa is the way we are," she said slowly. Then Jean-Desir's coolness was part of Guinea/Africa, too.

"*W*here *were* you, Mèt Sadrak?" Paulie asked in the hazy silence of late afternoon. "Where did you go after the FRAPH men came and closed the school?"

Mondestin, sitting up on the bow, answered for him. "Sadrak, *sé nèg mawon.*"

"What?" Paulie asked.

"A runaway. Person who will not be a slave."

"Can FRAPH make you a slave, Mèt Sadrak?"

"It's not like in the old days, Paulie," Sadrak said. "They don't put a chain on your ankle."

Paulie tried not to think of Jean-Desir's thumbs, tied together behind his back.

"Might as well," Mondestin put in.

"But the *macoutes* did hang around me, lean outside the school door. And they say I can teach this, but not that. They say I can teach things that are not

120

important, but I cannot discuss what *is* important. . . ." Sadrak spit into the water. "What kind of teacher would I be if I do what they say? I would be just the opposite of a teacher."

"And what is the opposite of a teacher?" Mondestin asked of nobody in particular.

"Not you, Mèt Sadrak," said Karyl, waking up. She yawned and shook her shoulders.

Paulie stared without seeing her. "So a *nèg mawon* is somebody who has to decide for themself how to be?" she asked, lost in her thoughts.

Sadrak nodded. "And in the old days, Paulie, the people who would not, could not let other people tell them how to live either killed themselves or ran to the mountains. These were men and women of Africa, and also men and women of the Taino people, who had been living in Haiti before white or black people came."

"Those Tainos were red people?" asked Karyl.

"More like Spanish-people color," said Sadrak. "Yellow-brown, with some red shine to it."

Sauveur was inspecting his forearm. He held it out next to Karyl's. Hers was dark brown. His was a yellow-red brown.

"You a Taino man, Sauveur?" Karyl asked him with a squeal of surprise.

Sauveur shook his head, smiling mysteriously.

"Then how come you so brassy color?"

"My granddaddy was married with a little woman come all the way from China."

"Noooo," said Karyl, shaking her head.

"Is true," said Sauveur. "You don't have to believe, but is true."

Paulie stretched her legs and frowned. "Sadrak?"

"Yes, Paulie."

"The *nèg mawon* and the Tainos, did they fight each other?"

"I don't know," said Sadrak. "Maybe they did, but I never heard tell of it. What I hear is that, together, in the mountains, they worked out the religion of *vodou*, and they fought against the people from Europe who were making all them people slaves."

"Did they ever win?" Karyl asked.

"Karyl!" said Mondestin.

"You forgot school already?" Sadrak asked. "And I risk my skin to teach you important stuff!"

Karyl hid her face in her hands and then peeped out.

"Okay," Sadrak continued. "Yes. Enriquillo was a Taino man and a *cacique* in Haiti, a big chief. He went to the mountains as a *nèg mawon* to fight the Spanish. Enriquillo did force the king of Spain to free the Taino people working on his plantation."

"Most were half-dead by then, teacher," Mondestin remarked. "Was too late for them."

"But the trying important, too, Mondestin," Sadrak said. Mondestin rubbed his neck.

"Another time, later on when it was the French who were ruling and putting people from Africa in slavery, Boukman did call together the *nèg mawon* and all the slaves rise up to join them and kill many French and throw the French out of Haiti—"

122

"*Paf!*" said Karyl, ramming a fist into one hand.

"Is there any other way to defeat the people who would make you into slaves, or do you only just have to kill them?" Paulie interrupted fiercely. Her head felt hot, and she wanted an answer.

They all rocked in silence for a while.

"If you ask me," Karyl said, "I think the best thing to do is just kill them."

Paulie looked at Lucille. Defeated, empty, Lucille stared unseeing at the water. The same woman who had said to her son, "Trying to stay alive by killing people is evil."

Paulie licked her lips and swallowed, wondering how to put the question in her mind into words. "If you don't want to kill," she said, "if killer is not what *you* want to be, and they making you kill, then you not free, you not deciding how to be. . . ." Paulie faltered anxiously. The habit of truth was harsh as sand in her mind.

"Paulie, look at me," said Sadrak. "If you put a gun in my hands, I will throw it in the sea. I am a *nèg mawon*, but I am not a killer. *Kenbe fèm*, standing firm for what you believe, that is action, too."

"Sure," said Karyl, disbelieving. "I say, best keep the gun."

Sauveur, lying in the bottom of the boat, lifted his hat off his face and joined the conversation. "Used to be, in the old days, a warrior was a good warrior because he was brave, and strong, and worked hard at it. My granddaddy was a stick-fighter, a good good stick-fighter. He never once kill anybody, but he always manage to prove he strongest. Now is a different story altogether. Because the gun do the killing. And to own a gun don't mean nothing: somebody give it to you to join some club like FRAPH, or you steal it, or you buy it. But none of that make you a good person, none of that take any braveness or work on your part. The biggest coward want the biggest gun. . . ." He ran his hand over his stubbled head and put his hat back over his face.

Sadrak made room for Paulie beside him and put her hands on the tiller.

"Hold this course, Paulie. Point just north of where the sun is going. Northwest, that's right. . . .

"I am thinking on your question," he said. "Is there a way to win free from slavery, to be a true part of Guinea/Africa, and to stay alive, all at once?"

Paulie looked out over the darkening waves, narrowing her eyes to shut out the glare of the setting sun. She nodded. Yes. That was her question. It was both scary and interesting to know that grown-ups like Mèt Sadrak and Mondestin and Lucille asked themselves the same question. The answer to such a big question was like the web Ti Malis had made in the story. It was beautiful, it was there, but you hardly ever did see it. With luck, you could glimpse it from time to time, when the light fell just right. . . .

"We each one seeking, best way we can," Sadrak added.

18

Lasyrenn

"Lasyrenn, Labalenn,
Chapo'm tonbe nan lanmè . . .
Mermaid spirit, whale spirit
I want to touch the water-mama
I reach to touch the water-mama
My hat falls in the sea . . ."

The day was just beginning. Paulie lay motionless in the bilge, listening to Adeline's song. The sky arched above them enormously high, hugely pink, with tiny clouds like shreds of lace high, high above, lit gold by first sun.

From where she lay, Paulie couldn't see Grann's face, but she could see that Grann held Lucille's hand and was stroking it as she sang.

"I want to touch the water-mama
Lasyrenn, the mermaid-whale,
I reach to touch . . ."

Adeline's gravelly voice held Lucille's yearning
as well as her own. Paulie heard it longing to be
beyond life, to know the deep, underwater part of
everything that maybe only the dead can know.

She turned her neck very slowly and rested her
forehead against the stout keel of *Seek Life*. Through
it, she could feel the vibrations of the boat, every
creak and pull. She could hear the gurgle that meant
they were still moving, the morning breeze pushing
them steadily to the northwest.

"**O**kay, Paulie, what you seeing?"

Paulie was in the bow, her chin pressed hard on
the bow post, staring into the water. She thought if
she tried enough she could make her eyes pierce
through like light, and see into the world below. She
wanted to see Lasyrenn, the mermaid, the whale-
goddess. She wanted to ask Lasyrenn questions big
as the ocean.

And now here was Sauveur trying to make conversation.

Paulie heaved a sigh. "You ever seen Lasyrenn,
Sauveur?"

"No," he said, settling in the bottom of the boat,
his legs stretched clear across and propped on the
gunwale next to her. "I never seen Lasyrenn yet, but

I do think about her night and day. . . ." He grinned and adjusted his hat.

"What does she look like, when you think about her?"

"Combing that long, long hair. Looking at me all fishy. One side black woman, one side white woman . . ." Sauveur gave a fake shiver. "Oo-ooh!"

Paulie smiled, but she turned back to the water. She couldn't listen to Sauveur's funniness right now. She had cast her concentration like a web down through the deep toward Lasyrenn, her calling, her longing, keeping the web taut. Any distraction could break it. In places the sun touched through the shifting green water, reaching down. . . .

A form rose to the surface, sudden and huge. It rose to meet Paulie, rushing toward her. Paulie caught her breath, lunging forward to meet the shape. Just under the surface, it flipped and plummeted deep, deep, leaving Paulie its heartbeat, as if it had kicked her in the chest with its powerful fluke. She reeled, off balance, full of fear and joy.

A hand grasped the back of her dress. It was Uncle's. "Go sit with you Grann, now, Paulie. We don't want to lose you in the sea." His hand closed over her shoulder, guiding her.

Paulie climbed over Sauveur and Gabriel and knelt trembling on the floor at the stern. She put her head and arms in Adeline's lap. She understood how Adeline yearned to join Lasyrenn, to let the big whale who knew everything carry her back to Guinea. She had touched that understanding, and she had almost fallen into it and drowned.

Paulie buried her face in Adeline's skirt, soaking it with big salt tears.

*T*he wind dropped, the sun climbed. Everything so bright and so hot. "Please, Uncle, can't we swim?" Karyl begged. "Boat not going anywhere. . . ."

Uncle just shook his head at her from where he held the tiller, rocking it sometimes to make it push them forward just a little.

White salt from the water he had poured over his head crusted around his mouth, and in the lines in his cheeks that went deep when he smiled. Paulie could feel how stiff his face had become. She handed him the jug half-full of fresh water, but he shook his head again.

"*W*e used to have land we could work . . . ," Adeline said suddenly.

"We used to have a place to fish from the rocks. . . .

"We had the peristyle, to make *seremoni*. We had the church. Small blue church by the waterfall. . . .

"We had chickens running around. Could kill one or two to feed the spirits. . . ." Adeline lapsed into silence, though her lips still moved.

So what do we have now? Paulie wondered.

"We alive, but not alive, because we have nothing to do," said Mondestin, his eyes closed under his hat.

"What we have now is just like what the *invisib* have, only we not invisible."

"Not invisible to ourselves. To everybody else we invisible," Sadrak added.

"When we separate from Belle Fleuve, when we cross over the waves and must leave our place, the place where we always live, is like when the *houngan* separate the body from the spirit-self. A *desouni*. Is like dying. . . ." Was it Uncle speaking now? Paulie couldn't tell anymore who was speaking.

"True. We got the energy of our spirit-self, but nothing to act upon. A person not alive if he is not planting something, digging something."

"Teaching something."

"Chopping something."

"Eating something. . . ."

When Paulie said this, Mèt Sadrak laughed, and so did Uncle.

Everyone sat in silence. The boat rocked very lightly on the waves. It seemed that they were not moving at all.

*P*aulie woke and climbed up into the night, up beside Grann.

"Don't you want to sleep, Grann? Is your turn," she whispered. Grann made room for her on the bench, gently pushed Lucille to lie down. Paulie shut her eyes tight, then opened them wide. It was still very dark, but the darkness held the possibility of light.

The greater darkness was below, the lesser darkness above. The place where darknesses met rocked and shifted.

The Bible in Grann's church told how in the beginning God separated the light from the dark.

"This is the beginning of the world, Grann? This is like the beginning of the world. . . ." More than anything, Paulie wanted just then to hear a voice she knew. A voice from the days she had lived on land, in the sunshine, to make this shifting misery into a story, so that she could hold it in her mind and not be held by it.

"What was it like, Grann, the beginning of the world?"

Adeline sat tight against Paulie, stiff as ever, and Paulie leaned against her, feeling the hum of her thoughts. Finally Grann spoke aloud.

"You know, Paulie . . . is not some long-time-ago thing, creation." She heaved a huge sigh and spread her fingers before her in the dark, whether to look at her hands or to call attention to the water below, Paulie couldn't tell.

"Mystery of being is now, Paulie. Open you eyes and look out there!"

Paulie opened her eyes obediently, though she didn't know she had closed them. All that vastness of sea and sky, no lights anywhere.

"That place out there look like a world where people belong? No. It don't look like that to me. Whale, maybe. Fish maybe. Bird up in the sky, maybe. But you and me, with all our worry? It don't seem like the place for us. . . ." Grann's voice was just a whisper, thin as a wood shaving. "But look here, Paulie. We here. We got spirit, we got understanding, we can ask. . . .

"The mystery that is the life of people is a mystery *now*." Adeline leaned forward. *"Henh!"* she added. "Look, you own self is mystery, not so?"

Paulie thought yes, she did feel it, so strange to be human and to think about it, while at the same time her bottom hurt from the hard bench of the boat, her stomach was queasy and hungry, her skin uncomfortable in her wet clothes. Her wondering came through her body, and also her body got in the way of her wondering. She felt Grann's hand, strong and warm, cupping her shoulder, yet she could feel it as bones. In a matter of days, Jean-Desir's hand would be just bones, and in a few years, it would be nothing at all.

Paulie licked salt from her lips, and swallowed. "Grann," she asked scratchily, "what happens to me when I die?"

The boat wallowed over a big swell, tilting as if to shrug them into the sea.

Adeline sat for a while in silence. Then she held her hands a few inches apart, palm facing palm. "Know how you like to look in Uncle's bit of mirror?"

Paulie felt her braids. *"Wi?"*

"Think, Paulie, that the girl you see in the mirror not just the picture, okay? Is also the studying, the asking question, the sadness, the trying hard, that go into this person we call Paulie. This real alive Paulie here.''

"But the mirror can break and all that gone. . . .''

"The mirror can break and the *picture* gone. Like the *macoutes* break the body of you friend Jean-Desir. That don't mean all the rest gone, too. When the body break, the rest come free of the body. When you dead—and you gonna die sometime, girl, like everybody—all that Paulieness come back to help the people that still living, and the new ones that be born.''

Paulie shifted around, lay down on one hip where Lucille had been, her head on Adeline's lap, keeping one hand tight around the gunwale of *Seek Life*.

Adeline kept her bony hand cupped around Paulie's shoulder, and after a while she spoke again, in the soft darkness. "Is not for nothing we live so hard, Paulie. Is not for ourself alone. And is not by ourself alone, either. Your great-great-granma come out of Africa on ship worse than this one, she helping you every step of the way.''

19

Rocked

 Paulie let herself be rocked. Again she lay in the bottom of *Seek Life*, her head on a bundle of clothes. Karyl was stretched out, too, with her feet propped on the sloping side of the boat. Paulie cradled Karyl's head on her stomach, and every time Karyl spoke, Paulie could feel the sound hum and tickle before she made any sense of it.

"I wish I had been more nice to Jean-Desir," Karyl was saying. "I was always so mean, teasing him about his foolishness. . . ."

Paulie put her hand against Karyl's face, felt the tears sliding down.

Paulie's stomach was empty. Her hipbones stuck

out sharp. It was the first time that she noticed that she had these bones, like the edge of a bowl low in her belly. It felt good to have Karyl's head there. She wondered what it would be like to hold a baby inside her, to have a child grow there.

"You think that is land or cloud, Sadrak?" Uncle asked, pointing to a low band of purplish black to the north of them.

Sadrak shook his head. "That is where land supposed to be, all right, but it looks too dark for land. . . ."

A fresh coldness hit the air. Paulie shivered, and Adeline reached down to untie bundles, to get out more clothes. The sky was covered now, whitish, and the sea was a brown-green that didn't hold light. The change in wind made the sail shift sides suddenly and heavily. Mondestin ducked fast not to get hit, and Uncle bit his lip, figuring how to steer.

"Looks like we'll have to go way up that way, then turn back east."

He set a new course that put the boat crossways to the waves. *Seek Life* plunged into them, wallowing, burying her nose. Sauveur moved to the stern.

Was it the tossing, twisting motion of the waves that was making her feel so sick, Paulie wondered, or was she just scared? The boat was fighting with the sea.

Paulie and Karyl sat side by side, low as they

could get, to hold the boat in the water. Karyl had her arm around Paulie's neck. Paulie braced them both, with hands against the bench and the centerboard trunk. Now and again a wave came over too far and they had to bail out water with the cup and a cut-off jug. It was better to be busy than to look at the wall of waves, brown and green.

Gabriel needed help to use the jug for a latrine.

"Hold the boy, Lucille, he's going to fall," Adeline cautioned, but Lucille did nothing, still stared into space as if dead. As Paulie looked at her, waiting to see if she could help her son, Lucille licked her lips and said one word, under her breath. Paulie thought it was "Sylvain," the name of Karyl's father. Paulie and Karyl held Gabriel, one on each side.

"Hurry up!" Karyl said impatiently, wrinkling her nose.

"Not so easy, is it?" said Paulie, and Uncle glanced at her kindly, his pirate headgear billowing up in the wind.

Sadrak was looking up ahead, and as the boat crested a wave, he broke into a shout. "Land! Uncle, you done it! There's land up there for sure."

Uncle stood tall, craning to see, the tiller between his knees. Next time the boat rose high, he broke into a grin, clapping Sadrak on the back, then Sauveur and Mondestin. Paulie felt tears spring to her eyes. She hugged Karyl and let herself know only then how frightened she was of the tossing water. She hugged Adeline and Lucille and Gabriel, too, pulled up Gabriel's pants, and emptied the jug overboard.

"What land you think it is?" she heard someone ask. Paulie didn't mind what land. Land was land.

*I*t took forever getting nearer. Four times Uncle had to swing the sail over, take another direction. "The wind keep changing its mind, Paulie. That's what the trouble is. Mostly the wind is blowing from the land, so we have to catch it whatever way we can."

"Wish we had a motor," said Karyl. "Motor can go anywhere you point it."

Uncle looked at her skeptically. "Motor require gasoline," he said. "The wind always come around, if you patient."

"Kanntes most dependable for folks like us, these days," said Sadrak, to ease Uncle's worry. Kannte was the brand name of a power generator that rarely worked and the name beach people gave to boats with no motors. "*Seek Life* the best Kannte I ever seen."

"Sorry," said Karyl, putting her head on Paulie's shoulder.

Uncle gave one of her braids a tug.

*P*aulie could see the land sometimes now, between the waves, low and gray, with shapes of brown and some dark green. "No mountains," she said to Adeline. "But the edge looks rough like maybe they have palm trees."

136

It seemed that the waves got bigger close to the land. Higher and more rough. Paulie was holding tight to the mast, watching Uncle scanning the line of fierce breakers for a way to bring the boat in to shore, when she heard a shout from Sauveur, saw his startled face, and turned to see what he was looking at.

Lucille had risen, was standing on the bench. As Paulie watched, Lucille stepped over the gunwale into the sea.

"Catch her!" yelled Uncle.

Adeline, grabbing at Lucille, was halfway over. Mondestin lunged for Adeline, and suddenly Paulie felt the boat flip, and was in the sea, underwater, cold, green salt stinging her eyes.

When she surfaced, the waves cut her view. She caught glimpses of bundles, an oar, the bottom of the boat, hands, heads. Close by, she saw a small head, just going down. Gabriel. She plunged toward him, dived under him, grabbed his shirt, and pushed him up to the surface. His jaws were locked tight, his eyes shut. Paulie blew water in his face, struggling to catch her own breath. Gabriel took a gulp of air.

She thought she saw Uncle trying to right the boat, others swimming, Sauveur's hat.

"Swim for land, Paulie! We not far out. . . ."

Locking her arm around Gabriel's shoulder, grasping his chin in her hand and forcing it out of the water, Paulie swam. It was awkward, hard to find direction. When she could look up, the shore was hidden by waves. She hit her foot on a rock, kicked back in anger, realized that a rock meant land.

Doggedly she swam on, until at last her foot touched sand.

20

Lòt Bò Dlo

The sky was gray-brown. The wind was blowing. The ocean still danced in choppy waves that ducked and jostled each other, like people in a crowd trying to see what they had done. Paulie sat on the wet gray sand. She looked at her feet. She held her hands beside them. Yes, her hands were long now, too. Long and thin and capable-looking. I saved a *ti moun*, she thought, a little person. Gabriel. She remembered the feel of Gabriel's sharp chin in her hand, how she had almost let go.

I didn't save Karyl, she thought. I didn't teach her to be friends with water.

She looked down the beach toward the others.

Lucille was sobbing, holding Gabriel close, her words pouring out to him, a loud endless babble that rose and fell in familiar cadences. Paulie heard Jean-Desir's name, Karyl's name, the word *defen* punching the flow of Lucille's words again and again, *defen* Jean-De, *defen* Karyl. The others surrounded Lucille, a wall of comfort, warming her, encouraging the healing flow of words with exclamations and groans of sympathy.

A few yards away, Karyl lay motionless and alone, her shoes and socks still on, the wind ruffling her Sunday dress. Paulie went to her. She knelt beside Karyl and straightened her dress. She put Karyl's feet side by side. Then she smoothed her friend's hair, arranged the braids, each with its bow, pulling them tall the way Paulie liked hers. Slowly she brushed sand from Karyl's hair with her fingers.

Through tears, Paulie saw a blur of light far down the beach. She blinked and realized that there was a road running low and dark along the sand. A line of cars was headed toward them. Wide, smooth-moving cars, with chrome shining across the fronts. Each had lights on its roof, blue lights that flashed, first one side, then the other.

*B*ecause the girl was dead, the police didn't take this group of refugees to the detention center, where men and women would have been separated. The police, talking quietly together, decided that Uncle was Lucille's husband, the child's father. The police assumed that all who stood together on the beach were one family, an old lady, four sons, a wife, two children. One policeman asked Uncle a question that might have been about kinship. Uncle nodded, saying, "*La-kou, wi.*"

The police led them to the three cars, opened the door to the first one. Lucille and Gabriel slid in first, across the long seat. Then Uncle got in, holding Karyl's body on his knees, holding her as if she were still alive, though Paulie could imagine the cold, wet weight of her. Paulie loved Uncle, that he could hold Karyl so. The policeman closed the door with a firm slam. Paulie could make out Uncle, inside. Right where his face looked out at her, she could also see the reflection of her own face. Because he was brave and she was his niece, she turned without protest and got in the next car with Adeline and Mondestin, though she was scared of the white policemen and had no idea where the big car would take them.

Mondestin, who had towed Karyl to the beach too late, sat with his face in his hands. His back shook. Adeline sat very straight beside him. Paulie wedged her cold hands between her knees, to warm them. Her dress was wet, and sand scraped her back.

*T*he kind people who took them in at the refugee center were surprised when Paulie asked them to put through a telephone call for her. The number was a local one, a Miami radio station. They were surprised that she knew the name of a reporter, and that he came to the phone to talk to a girl who was almost a child and who spoke no English.

Paulie herself was surprised to be talking to Anton Bertis through a plastic telephone handle. She had never held a receiver in her hand before, but she could tell that the voice that came from it was his. Haltingly, she told him about the crossing, about the landing.

"What can I do to help, Paulie? Is there anything I can do to help?"

"You can tell people about Karyl, about Jean-Desir. Whatever truth you know, even just a little piece," she said, thinking out loud.

"I can do that," said Anton Bertis, but his voice had no courage.

Paulie thought hard. "Tomorrow or the next day we will have a service. We will pray and call spirit. Invite people on the radio. Tell them to come be with us, to cry and beat drums and shout and sing loud."

"How would that help?" Bertis asked. "Does crying help? Do drums help?" His voice was like a bird caught inside a hut, trying to find a way out.

"But if they come and cry and open themself to the spirit . . . ," she said.

"What, Paulie? What spirit?"

"Understanding," Paulie said. "*Konesans*. Somebody might get one glimpse—like a spiderweb in the sun. Then they would know what to do next. . . ."

Paulie was still thinking about this, the plastic

receiver in her hand, her eyes looking at the wall of the refugee center, when Lucille came and hung up the phone. Lucille put a blanket around Paulie. She took her to a cot, helped her lie down, and tucked a pillow gently under her head. For a minute, Lucille kept her strong hand, still smelling of fish, on Paulie's head.

THE HISTORY AROUND THE STORY

TONIGHT, BY SEA takes place in 1993. The years 1991 through 1994 were very hard for people in Haiti.

Most Haitians are rich in imagination, courage, and *demele*, ways to get along and help one another. But most Haitians are extremely poor in other ways: no food, no water, no shelter, and up until very recently, no government protection.

The poor in Haiti have no money. In Haiti a factory worker makes about fifteen cents an hour, and a farm worker makes even less. Food is not cheap. Oranges and bananas grow on trees in Haiti, but the trees almost always belong to someone else. For many years Haiti has been run by the rich, for the rich. These rich include Americans, stockholders and company executives, many of whom have never been in Haiti.

In 1990, the Haitian people, the poor majority, decided to change this situation. They elected as president and spokesperson a young priest, one of themselves, who had long worked among the poorest in Haiti. This new president, Jean-Bertrand Aristide, spoke of moving Haiti "from inhuman misery to a dignified poverty," of making Haiti a country where every person could have one meal a day, where everyone would have clean water to drink, where everyone had some work and would get paid enough to keep a roof overhead.

This does not seem like much, but it required changes. The wealthy would have to begin paying taxes. The factory owners would have to increase wages, perhaps up to fifty cents an hour, and make some improvements in working conditions. The owners of the big farms, the sugar plantations and agribusinesses, would have to pay their workers a modest minimum wage.

Most of all, the rich, the "owner" class, who were used to thinking that government was for their private benefit, would have to realize that government was for everybody and that they couldn't be the only ones to make decisions anymore.

They didn't like it. Together, the rich of Haiti, some of the military, and some from outside Haiti who had factories, farms, or interests there, including many American businesses, put so much pressure on President Aristide that, seven months after he became president, he was toppled in a coup d'état.

Military leaders took over. For the next three years, from 1991 through 1994, soldiers and hired thugs beat up, raped, killed, and stole from any Aristide supporter they could find. Four hundred thousand people went into hiding inside Haiti, living in fields or in caves, eating garbage and leaves and roots. Many thousands of people built small boats and left the country by sea.

But the more the Haitian people suffered, the more determined many became not to give in, not to accept being "owned" by the rich and powerful.

Little by little, the rest of the world started to pay attention to the Haitian people. Some people in the United States were angry when they found out that, instead of helping the Haitian people with reforms, U.S. companies, backed by the Commerce Department, the CIA, and parts of the U.S. Army, had helped the rich overthrow Aristide and destroy what he stood for.

American workers, already anxious at seeing so many jobs go overseas, began to realize that companies that depended for labor on workers in countries like Haiti, with no enforced minimum wage, had a vested interest in keeping these countries poor and were perpetuating slavery.

Concerned people in the United States, especially Black leaders who felt a historic imperative to prevent new forms of slavery, put pressure on the U.S. government to change its policies, to support the Haitian people. Slowly, the U.S. government has responded. Although at the time of this writing in late 1994, there is evidence that some branches of the U.S. government, such as the CIA, are still supporting antidemocratic forces in Haiti, there are also signs of hope. President Clinton has sent U.S. troops to help reinstate President Aristide. Many Americans are seeing Haiti firsthand. President Aristide's proposed reforms, including enforcement of minimum wage laws, are being considered by the international community.

This is not the end of the story. The last five years have shown that the future of Haiti will depend, not only on the hard work of the Haitian people and of President Aristide, but also on common people in the United States, who need to continue pushing the U.S. government and the global business community toward fairer, more helpful policies.

GLOSSARY

ak tou kò With the whole body. Wholeheartedly.

amistad Spanish for friendship. A slave ship called *Amistad* was taken over by its "cargo" in 1848, as it made its way to a port in Cuba. The Africans on board sailed the ship as far as Connecticut, where it was captured by a U.S. warship. The Africans were tried for murder and theft. Their trial became a major court challenge to slavery. John Quincy Adams defended Joseph Cinque, leader of the Africans.

Aristide, Jean-Bertrand A Salesian priest whose work has been largely with the poor in Haiti, Aristide was elected president of Haiti in 1990 by an overwhelming majority. Seven months into his presidency, he was ousted by a military coup d'état (see "The History around the Story," p. 145). In this book, Aristide is often referred to as Titid.

balanse Swing or sway.

Bondye God. *Bondye bon*: God is good.

bonswa Good evening.

Bouki A fat, greedy bumpkin in Haitian folklore.

cacique Creole: *kasik*. A Taino chief within the cooperative society that prevailed on the island of Ayiti before the arrival of Columbus. Both men and women served as *caciques*.

chache lavi (or chèche lavi) To seek life.

coup d'état Creole: *koudeta*. An overthrow of the legitimate government, usually by the military.

Creole (Kreyol)   The language of the majority in Haiti, Creole is based on several African languages and French.

defen   Dead or defunct. Among country people in Haiti, it is customary to refer to someone who has died by their first name preceded by the word *defen*. For instance, after Marie's death, she is called *defen* Marie.

desouni   Separation or dis-unifying. *Desouni* refers to a ceremony in the *vodou* religion in which the spirit of someone who has died is recognized as having come free of the body.

djab   Devil.

fèt   Party, celebration.

FRAPH   An acronym for *Front pour l'Avancement et le Progrès d'Haiti*, a paramilitary terrorist group that oppressed the Haitian people during the years of President Aristide's exile. The word as pronounced in Creole means to strike a blow.

Gede   In the *vodou* religion, there are many *lwa*, or spirits, archetypes of the energy each person has within. Gede is the spirit who most personifies humor, especially sexual humor. He is also considered the protector of children, and is closely associated with death.

grandon   A big shot.

Guinea   Creole: *Ginen*. Used in Haiti to refer to Africa as a homeland, also to a spiritual home, and by extension to a state of rapturous awareness, particularly for a person of African origin.

houngan   A coordinator of the *serviteurs*, or those who serve the spirits in the *vodou* religion.

invisib   Invisible. Often refers to those who have died and become all spirit.

kleren   Raw rum.

kok chante   The rooster sings; wake-up call. The rooster is a symbol of the populist coalition that elected President Aristide. The rooster is often painted on walls and buses in Haiti as a symbol of hope.

kòkòt   An affectionate term for a little girl.

kombit (or koumbit) Originally meant a farming work group; now, any cooperative work group.

konesans   Knowledge or understanding, with special connotations of spiritual connectedness.

kwi   A gourd bowl or dipper.

lakou   Courtyard, with a special meaning of extended family: often, in Haiti, extended families live in several houses grouped around a yard where people cook and visit.

lambi   Conch shell, used as a horn to call for the rising of slaves in the rebellion against the French colonialists and, since, for political rallying.

Lasyrenn   The Mermaid. Lasyrenn is a female spirit associated with the West African Mammy Water, and with intuition. She is also called Labalenn, which means the Whale.

Lavalas   The flood. In *vodou* religion, as in the Old Testament, a cleansing power. Lavalas was the name given to the populist coalition that brought Aristide to the presidency. In the aftermath of the coup d'état that ousted Aristide in 1991, thousands of people associated with the Lavalas movement, including many schoolteachers and peasant leaders, were persecuted and killed.

Legba   A *vodou lwa*, or spirit, guardian of the spirit world, one who stands at the crossroads and must be persuaded to grant access to those who would cross.

lòt bò dlo   The other side of the water.

lwa   A spirit that epitomizes some aspect of human personality. The major *lwa* are Legba, Erzuli, Damballa, Gede, Agwe, Ogun, and Azaka. There are many others.

macoute   Originally, the term *tonton macoute* meant an uncle with a sack on his back. In the old days, this was an image used to frighten children, a bogeyman. The dictator François Duvalier organized a private army of thugs whose role was to terrorize any opposition. Deliberately sinister and anonymous, they took the name of *tontons macoutes*. Today, *macoute* is a word used for bad guy, and *macoutisme* refers to rule through terror.

madansara   Finches that travel in flocks, and also market women, who often travel great distances together.

Mèt   A term of respect for teachers.

moto, motosiklet   Motorcycle.

msye   Mister.

nèg mawon   Runaway slave. By extension, a revolutionary, or someone who refuses to comply with an oppressive system.

onnè   Honor: a greeting. The response: *respè*, respect.

oslè   A game like jacks played with pig vertebrae.

petro   A group of spirits in *vodou*. The drumming style used to call them is urgent, loud, and insistent.

Port-au-Prince   Creole: Pot-o-Prins. The capital city of Haiti.

poto mitan   The center pole used to hold up the roof in a *vodou peristil*, or worship house. The spirits sometimes enter the *peristil* by way of the *poto mitan*. For that reason, a *poto mitan* also means, by extension, a charismatic person, or a person through whom riches of the spirit are made available to others.

respè Respect. The second half of the greeting *onnè-respè*.

sans-maman A good-for-nothing. Literally, a person without a mother.

section chief A political position at the local level, much abused under the dictatorship and during Aristide's exile.

seremoni A *vodou* ceremony to serve the spirits, often involving singing, dancing, preparing a feast, drawing designs on the floor with cornmeal. Sometimes a rooster or other farm animal is sacrificed for the feast. Sometimes during a *seremoni* one of the spirits (see *lwa*) will possess and speak through someone at the gathering.

Si Dye vle If God wishes.

simpatik Likable, understanding.

Taino The original inhabitants of the island of Hispaniola, which is now shared by the Dominican Republic and Haiti.

Ti Malis A clever trickster in Haitian folklore, much like Anansi the Spider or Br'er Rabbit.

ti moun Child or children.

Titid A widely used and affectionate nickname for President Aristide.

tonnè Thunder: a mild expletive.

vèvè *Vodou* symbol, often a symmetrical design.

Vodou A religious practice for honoring spirit, sometimes called voodoo.

zetwal Star.